MURPHY'S AMBUSH

Also by Gary Paulsen

Murphy's Stand (with Brian Burks, coauthor)
Murphy's Herd
Murphy's Gold
Murphy

MURPHY'S AMBUSH

Gary Paulsen and Brian Burks

Walker and Company
New York

First published in the United States of America in 1995 by Walker
Publishing Company, Inc.

Published simultaneously in Canada by Thomas Allen & Son Canada,
Limited, Markham, Ontario

Library of Congress Cataloging-in-Publication Data
Paulsen, Gary.
Murphy's ambush / Gary Paulsen and Brian Burks.
p.   cm.
ISBN 0-8027-4149-5
I. Burks, Brian. II. Title.
PS3566.A834M83   1995
813'.54—dc20   95-1769
CIP

Printed in the United States of America

2   4   6   8   10   9   7   5   3   1

MURPHY'S AMBUSH

CHAPTER 1

SHERIFF AL MURPHY sat back in his chair and propped his feet up on the desk. He took the makings from his shirt pocket and meticulously rolled a cigarette while waiting for his second pot of morning coffee to boil.

But his thoughts weren't on the cigarette or the coffee. He was thinking about Christine McCormick, as he often did.

Steps sounded on the plank boardwalk in front of the jail and the door burst open. Skeet Ames, a small wiry man with an age-wrinkled face, rushed in.

"Sheriff, you better be gettin' on over to the Doc's. Travis Price just come in. He's been shot up some."

Murphy grabbed his hat and gun belt from a peg on the wall.

"He's carryin' an arrow too."

"An arrow?" Murphy brushed past Skeet and half ran down Turrett, New Mexico's, main street. At the end, he turned toward a small adobe house that served as Doc Woods's home and office. A small sorrel mare, lathered with sweat, stood loose in the yard, nibbling at the grass. Murphy noticed the dark blotches on the horse's bare back. He could tell it was blood. Travis Price's blood.

A few men were gathered on the veranda, talking. When they saw Murphy, they moved to the side, allowing him room to pass. Murphy opened the door, stepped into the hall, and opened the office door to his right. He knew his way around. What was now referred to as the Turrett County war had given him enough wounds to become more familiar with the place than he cared to remember.

Bernard Gibson had started the trouble, killing Christine's brother to try to gain the McCormick Mercantile's contract to supply beef to Fort Crosston. But with the help of Skeet and Moses, Murphy had put an end to Gibson and his murderous greed.

Price lay on a long, high wooden table; Doc Woods hovered above him, busily probing into a hole just below the man's collarbone with a thin steel rod and wire loop. Murphy stepped to the opposite side of the table, and the old, white-haired doctor spoke without taking his eyes from his work.

"The arrow shaft's over there." The doctor nodded toward a counter at the end of the room. Murphy walked over to it as Doc went on. "Been five years or more since I worked on an arrow wound. Figured Apache troubles was over and I'd never have to do it again. Guess I was wrong.

"Not really much else I can tell you. Travis never said anything. He fell unconscious when we took him off his horse. A bullet creased his skull and another one went through his leg just above the knee. This arrow wound's what worries me the most. They're bad to get infected."

Doc Woods grunted and jerked the steel rod out of the hole. A large, bloody arrowhead was in the wire loop at the end of it.

"He's lost a lot of blood. If that doesn't kill him, he might pull through. Too bad this happened to him. As long as I've known Travis Price, he's been all right. Takes good care of his family and ranch, and never bothers anyone."

Murphy laid the arrow shaft back on the counter and started for the door. "Thanks, Doc. I hope he makes it."

Skeet almost ran into Murphy in the hall. "Well?"

"I don't know," Murphy kept walking toward the front door. "He's unconscious. I'm going out to his place."

Skeet caught up with Murphy in the yard. "I'm goin' with you. I'll go and get Moses. You're liable to need us for sure."

Murphy stopped. "You and Moses don't have a freight run today?"

"Naw. We don't leave for the fort till tomorrow mornin'."

"All right, then. Hitch up a buckboard and meet me out there."

"Me and Moses don't need a wagon. You ain't the only one what can ride a horse, you know. Why, I was ridin' broncs before you was born. That's the trouble with you young—"

Murphy interrupted, raising his hand. "Bring the wagon, Skeet. I hope like the devil that we don't need it."

CHAPTER 2

MURPHY WENT TO the small corral he'd built behind the jail and caught and saddled his big, muscular, mouse-colored *grulla*. He opened the gate and mounted. The horse immediately lowered his head and danced sideways, acting like he was going to buck. Murphy smiled at the horse's playful antics.

The slick *grulla* bore little resemblance to the plodding, worn-out skeleton that had aimlessly carried Murphy toward Turrett a year ago. But then, the horse wasn't the only one who'd changed.

After the death of his wife Midge, a few years earlier, Al Murphy had drifted from place to place, a hollowed-out, half-starved wreck of a man who had turned to whiskey to ease his grief until the pain and bleeding in his stomach had forced him to all but quit. Life held no meaning as Murphy traveled on, unknowingly searching for a reason to go on living.

Several miles outside of Turrett, fate and circumstances worked together to help him find that reason. He stumbled on the tail end of the murder of Jake McCormick, and through a series of events, Murphy helped Christine save the family business after her brother's death.

The local sheriff died during the ensuing conflict between the two warring mercantiles. Having heard of Murphy's previous law-enforcement experience, the town leaders urged Murphy to accept the job. Skeet Ames, a McCormick freight mule skinner, and Moses Coffin, ex-soldier and blacksmith, became Murphy's friends and deputies.

4

The battles were over now, and Sheriff Al Murphy's wounds had healed. Other than an occasional saloon brawl, some rustling, and a few fights over water rights—all things that were common to every frontier settlement—Turrett had been quiet for months.

In appreciation for their efforts in the war, Christine had made Murphy, Skeet, and Moses part owners of the McCormick Mercantile. Skeet and Moses, at Murphy's urging, quit their law jobs and looked after their interest in the store by driving the freight wagons to Fort Crosston, eighty miles to the east.

Murphy stayed on as sheriff, which was the one thing he'd found that he was good at. For the first time in a long time, he felt that he wanted to stay put. Being a store clerk or mule skinner didn't appeal to him, and except for ranching, something he hadn't done much of, there was little else he could find to do.

The job and Christine had given his life a new focus. He now looked forward to the future while taking pride in the recent accomplishments of the past.

Christine McCormick stood on the steps in front of the rough, wood-plank mercantile, gazing down the street toward the jail. Skeet had told her about Travis Price, and she knew Murphy would be riding by on his way to the Price ranch.

She was an unusually pretty woman in her mid-twenties, with a gracefully slender, yet full figure, long blond hair, and large green eyes. But it was more her manner than her looks that set her apart from other women. A certain way she held her head and moved that might be seen as arrogance by anyone who didn't know her. Those who did, knew better.

The McCormick ranch lay eight miles northwest of Turrett. Christine's folks had homesteaded and built the place, but they'd died years ago, leaving Christine and Jake to run it. After Jake died, Christine found that she had no choice but to try and fill his shoes, taking care of the things he'd always handled at the ranch and store. Sarah McCormick, Jake's widow, and their seven-year-old son, Billy, lived at the ranch with Christine. Sarah inherited Jake's part of the ranch and store, but let Christine run the business end of everything while she took care of Billy, the home place, and did all the cooking for the ranch hands.

Murphy turned the corner, and Christine watched him approach, approving of the way he held his tall, lean, raw-boned frame straight in the saddle. She was pleased with the change in Murphy, especially in the last few months—it was becoming harder for her to remember him as the broke, gun-toting, empty-eyed saddle tramp who had drifted into her life a year ago.

He'd gained twenty-five pounds, but could still stand a few more. His clothes were always clean and he wore the best hat and boots money could buy. Christine McCormick was no silly schoolgirl. She was a smart, mature woman who knew that a big part of the change in Murphy revolved around her, and like Murphy, she too looked forward to the future.

The *grulla* pawed the ground, slung his head, and snorted in disgust at having to stop. Christine stepped to the ground and looked into Murphy's light-blue eyes.

"Skeet told me about Travis. It's hard to believe. The Apaches have been quiet on the reservation for four or five years. I'm afraid to even think of what you might find out there. Please be careful."

Murphy nodded and touched the brim of his hat. "You know I will."

Two hours later, Murphy topped a cedar- and piñon-jotted rocky ridge. The August sun was already hot and the *grulla's* chest was lathered, though the twelve miles of travel had done little to tire the horse. Below, in a narrow, grassy valley with a stream running through the middle, lay the Price ranch.

Murphy let the *grulla* pick his way down the slope. The uneasy feeling he'd had since leaving Turrett grew into a tight knot in the pit of his stomach. Months of chasing Apaches as an army scout during the Indian Wars had taught him what to expect if a band of renegade Apaches had indeed struck the Price homestead. He could only hope that Travis had been riding somewhere away from home when attacked. But that wasn't likely. If he had been, his horse would have been saddled.

Murphy remembered the last time he'd seen the Prices, a month, no, nearly two months ago. Skeet had overheard some barroom talk about a week-old shooting that had occurred out at Clyde Harrelson's Bar X, a large ranch about eleven miles south and a little west of the Price homestead.

When Murphy heard the news, he left for the ranch immediately, annoyed that should the account be true, no one from the Bar X had notified him.

He arrived at the ranch headquarters in midafternoon. Clyde Harrelson stepped out from under the blacksmith shed to greet him. He was a short, stocky, blond man with a wide, flat face, and wearing a ruffled brown suit. Another man, a tall, lanky fellow Murphy had never seen before, followed him close behind.

Murphy stepped off the *grulla*.

"You're a fair piece from home. Are you lost, Sheriff?" Clyde asked.

"No, I think I know where I'm at." Murphy was in no mood for pleasantries and he went right to the point of his visit. "I understand there's been a shooting here. Why wasn't I notified?"

The statement and question obviously rattled Clyde, yet it was amazing how quickly he was able to regain his composure. "Why . . . why yes. I wish it hadn't happened. I did my best to stop it."

"What happened?"

"Do you know a cowboy named Ben Simson?" Clyde asked.

Murphy shook his head.

"Well," Clyde went on. "He was one of my ranch hands. He drank too much and wouldn't work, and I had to fire him. A few days later he came back, drunk, with a pistol in his hand. He tied his horse in front of the house and stood out there, yelling for me to come out and face him.

"Sandy, here, my foreman"—Clyde gestured to the man standing to the side and slightly behind him—"and me stepped out to meet him. I did my best to quiet him, to get him to put his gun up. He pulled down on me and I had no choice but to shoot him."

"I saw the whole thing, Sheriff," Sandy broke in, his lips parting over broken teeth and a cynical light in his eyes. "It was self-defense, clear and simple."

"Why didn't one of you ride to town and report it?"

"Like he said"—Clyde pointed at Sandy—"it was self-defense. I'm not proud of what happened, but there didn't seem to be a reason to get the law involved. No law was broken. We just buried him and went on with livin'."

Murphy's temper soared at the statement. "You don't decide what pertains to the law in Turrett County, I do!" A moment later Murphy shifted his gaze to Sandy. "Were there any other witnesses?"

Clyde answered fast, a little too fast, making sure Sandy had no time to respond. "No . . . the hands . . . all of 'em were up north in the Dripping Springs pasture, branding. Even the cook was gone."

Murphy shrugged, doubting the story. "Show me where you buried Simson."

The three walked a few hundred yards east of the house to a small, fenced-in cemetery. Outside the fence was a fresh mound of dirt and no marker.

No one spoke. Murphy considered digging up the

corpse to be sure there were no bullet holes in the back, but decided against it. Better than a week had passed and chances were the body was too badly decomposed for him to be able to tell much.

He mounted the *grulla*. With apparently no other witnesses, he had no alternative but to take Clyde and Sandy's word for what had happened. Though he didn't like it, there was nothing else to do but leave without making an arrest.

He looked down at Clyde. "If there's another shooting on this ranch, I better hear about it quick, or you're going to jail for hindering the duties of a peace officer, obstruction of justice, and anything else I can think of.

"I remind you"—Murphy glared at Sandy—"I'm the law in Turrett County, at least for now."

Clyde managed a smile. "Sure you are. We just weren't thinkin' right. Won't happen again, I promise you that."

Murphy nodded, turned his horse, and spurred it into a canter. It was late in the evening when he'd stopped off at the Price place. Travis was coming out of the barn with a pailful of milk. His two little girls, Anna and Lorie, were running in circles around him, laughing. On seeing Murphy, Travis gestured toward the house with the pail.

"You got here just right, Sheriff. The missus is 'bout got supper on. You'll stay and eat with us, won't ya?"

Murphy smiled. He really didn't know Travis well. Over the past year he had only seen him and his family a couple of times, yet on each occasion they treated him well.

He stepped down, tied his horse to the hitching rail in front of the house, and turned to Travis. "A man'd be a fool to turn down your wife's cooking."

Travis grinned. "Don't I know it." He moved to the door and opened it. "Mama, we got company. The sheriff is here."

Mrs. Price, who was five months pregnant, stepped in the doorway. She was young, perhaps in her late twenties, with wide, dark eyes, brown, wavy hair, and a few freckles on her nose. "Come on in here. I made a big pot of venison stew and was wondering how on earth we were going to eat it all."

Murphy stepped inside behind her. Travis motioned to a chair at one end of the homemade plank table. "Sit down there."

He set the milk pail on a counter, took two tin cups off a shelf, and put one in front of Murphy. "Coffee'll be done directly. What brings you out here this late in the day?"

"Business." Murphy explained his visit to the Bar X and what he'd learned about the shooting of Ben Simson. Travis didn't comment, just listened while staring at his empty cup and gently rolling it between his fingertips. Soon Mrs. Price and the girls had the table set and a heaping portion of steaming stew in every bowl.

"Lorie," she said, "will you say the blessing?"

Lorie glanced nervously at their guest, then bowed her head. Murphy had never seen two girls any cuter. They both looked like their mother, and if it wasn't for their difference in age, it would be easy to mistake them for twins.

Lorie began. "Dear Lord, thank you for this food, and . . . and thank you for the sheriff who come by to see us. Please watch over the baby inside mama and take care of our new calf. In Jesus' name, Amen."

CHAPTER 3

THE PRICE RANCH house and barn were three hundred yards away when Murphy dismounted, pulled his .40-60 Winchester out of the scabbard, and tied the *grulla* to a yucca bush. There was a remote chance that the Indians were still around, and even if they weren't, he didn't want his horse disturbing any of the tracks in the area.

The windmill by the barn squeaked lazily in the breeze as Murphy stepped slowly into the ranch yard. The front door of the windowless, two-room cabin the Prices called home was open, and his anxiety increased.

He went to the barn first. In one of the stalls he found the family milk cow. Her throat had been slit and her hindquarters and tenderloin removed. Her calf was gone.

Reluctantly, Murphy left the barn and moved toward the house, his rifle poised ready in his hands, though it was obvious the raiding party was gone. His hands trembled at the door and his breath grew short. Finding the milk cow had further heightened his suspicion that he would not find any survivors.

He stepped in, waiting a moment for his eyes to adjust to the dimness. The room was a mess. Dishes, clothes, and straw bedding were scattered everywhere. Murphy stepped into the other room. Mrs. Price sat in a corner with her head back and eyes open. Two arrows were in her chest. She was dead.

"My God," Murphy whispered, stepping back. It took a minute and the thought of the Prices' two little girls to make him go back in.

He found the girls in the opposite corner from their

mother, where their nightgown-clad bodies had been thrown. Blood stained the walls around them and pooled on the floor. Both their tiny heads had been bashed in.

Murphy rushed outside. He doubled over and vomited. After he had brought up his morning coffee the dry heaves came. Then he went to the trough by the windmill and washed his face and hands, somehow thinking that the cool water would wash away the stark reality of the still morning.

Death wasn't new to Al Murphy. He'd seen more of it than most men. But not even the extreme violence and cruelty of the Indian Wars had been able to harden him against the brutal, senseless killing of women and children. Especially a woman and two small children he knew.

Murphy stood up. The water had helped and he felt better. His thoughts turned to Skeet and Moses. They would arrive soon. He started slowly back toward the cabin, intending to carry the three bodies outside and cover them. He didn't want Skeet and Moses to live with the haunting memory of seeing what he'd seen.

The gut-wrenching task finished and still no wagon in sight, Murphy rolled and lit a cigarette, then carefully studied the tracks in the yard and around the barn. It hadn't rained in a week, and in the powdery, churned-up dirt it was difficult to tell which horse tracks were fresh. Many of the tracks could have been made by ranch horses coming to water.

However, several men's footprints showed clearly. Some wearing boots, others moccasins. Reservation Indians were known to trade for boots whenever they could, so the tracks didn't reveal much. Murphy circled behind the barn. His initial nausea had been replaced by fierce anger.

Why would anyone do this to the Prices?

The family undoubtedly had little worth stealing. Even so, Murphy believed theft must have been the motive.

A small band of hungry, young Apache renegades who

had probably come across the ranch more by accident than design. If they were able to make off with a few horses, a gun or two and a little beef, it was worth it.

Like many tribes, the Apaches believed they were a superior people and that all others existed only to serve their needs. The death of a white woman and two children was of little consequence—they shouldn't have been on land the Apaches claimed in the first place.

Finding more boot and moccasin prints, Murphy widened his circle, finally locating where the band of Indians had tied their horses in a thick stand of junipers a couple of hundred yards from the house. He couldn't be sure, but there appeared to have been close to a dozen ponies tied there, most of them the mustang variety, with small, unshod hooves.

Three trails led away from the spot. One where the Apaches had walked their horses in, another where they'd left at a trot, and a third that showed their horses moving at a dead run toward the homestead.

Murphy followed the latter, confused by it. If the renegades attacked on horses, why did they bother to stop and tether them in the first place? He followed the trail to the dusty ranch yard, where he lost it among the other tracks, then picked it up again in the short grass south of the house. If the trail held its present course, it was going straight for Turrett.

Some, if not all, of the Apaches must have chased Travis Price. When they hadn't been able to catch him before he reached town, they may have doubled back and ransacked the place, killing Mrs. Price and the two girls.

The sound of a squeaky wagon reached Murphy, and he started back for the cabin. He reached the house in time to see the buckboard, pulled by two small brown mules, swing into the yard. Moses Coffin, a six-foot-six, close to three-hundred-pound black man, sat on the wagon seat next to the small wiry-framed Skeet.

Moses would take this hard, Murphy knew. Besides the fact that he, like most everyone in the county, knew the Prices, the big man's heart matched his size. Unless riled, Moses was the gentlest, kindest man Murphy had ever known.

"Whoa, you mules," Skeet hollered. The buckboard lurched to a stop and Skeet set the brake.

"Well, what'd you find? You can see I brung the wagon like you said. Ain't you . . ."

The look in Murphy's eyes silenced Skeet. He had known Murphy long enough to be able to tell that something was wrong.

Then Moses and Skeet saw the three bodies lying side by side in front of the house. The raiders had taken all the bedding in the house, so Murphy had had to wrap the bodies in tow sacks he'd found in the barn.

The wagon creaked loudly as Moses shifted his weight and stepped to the ground. He moved between the two girls, knelt, and removed the burlap from the smaller one's face.

"Anna," his voice quivered. He looked around at Murphy and Skeet. "Look—look what they done to sweet little Anna Price."

Murphy looked at his feet. Skeet sat on the wagon seat without moving a muscle. Moses put the covering back and carefully smoothed it out with trembling fingers, then stood and backed away from the bodies, stopping beside Murphy. His eyes were watery. "The Apaches done this?"

Murphy nodded. "Looks that way."

"I be goin' after 'em. I be goin' now. Them . . ." He pointed at the bodies, choked up, and wiped his eyes with the back of his hand. "Them baby girls ain't never hurt nobody. Them Apaches gonna pay for this. Lord help me, they's goin' to pay."

"No, Moses," Murphy said. "I'm going after them. I need you and Skeet to take the bodies back to the Doc's. He'll get them ready. As hot as it is, they'll have to be buried this evenin' or early tomorrow morning."

Skeet stepped down from the wagon.

Moses shook his head. "Skeet can haul 'em. My gun's under the wagon seat. I be goin'."

"You haven't got your horse with you and neither of the mules are big enough to carry you."

"I knew to bring my horse. Wished I had. But I can walk. I walked in the army."

Murphy knew how stubborn his friend could be, once he set his mind on something, and Murphy really didn't want him going. The grain-fed *grulla* was in perfect condition, and the sheriff planned to travel fast, very fast.

"We're wasting time, Moses. I know how you feel and I feel the same, but you'll only slow me down and I won't leave you behind.

"You and Skeet have to haul the freight to Fort Crosston tomorrow. I need you to tell the major there what's happened. He'll send out troops."

Then Murphy lied. "This is a military matter. The band of Apache renegades had to have broken out of a Federal Indian Reservation. Besides, there's too many of them for us to fight. I'm only going to follow and keep track of their movements so the army will have an easier time finding them. It's the military, Moses—the army has to handle this. It's out of our hands."

"Murphy's right," Skeet chimed in. "Times a-wastin' and there's another thing. Who knows where them Apaches is headed? We might run across them on our way to the fort and it'd take the both of us to fight 'em off."

Moses' speech was slow, and like Skeet, he had no education, but there was nothing dumb about him. He knew that Fort Crosston was eighty miles from Turrett and that it would take three days in the slow-moving freight wagons to reach it. The troops couldn't get back to Turrett in less than another two, giving the Apaches a five-day lead.

Still, the part about it being a military matter did make some sense, and Skeet was right, the Apaches probably would hit the freight wagons if they were in the vicinity.

"Okay. I be goin' on back to town with Skeet. But I ain't forgettin' what them Apaches done. One way or the other, they gonna pay."

CHAPTER 4

THE *GRULLA* MOVED along in the same steady, ground-eating canter he'd been in for two hours. The tracks of the Indian ponies were easy to follow and Murphy no longer had to guide the horse. He knew to stay on the trail.

A few miles farther and the horse paused of his own accord in the same place the Apaches had stopped. Ahead were miles of seemingly endless plains, and in the distance, barely visible through the sun's glare, was the headquarters of the Bar X ranch.

Murphy took a drink from his canteen, removed his hat, and wiped his brow with his shirtsleeve. The *grulla's* chest and flanks were heavily lathered and his breathing harsh, but it didn't worry Murphy. Grain, lots of it, caused that. The horse would quit sweating before the day was over.

The tracks and the missing heads of the thick grama grass showed that the Indians had stopped for quite a while, allowing their mounts to graze. Afterward, they'd headed to the right, skirting the edge of the open plateau to avoid being seen. If they had a plan and knew where they were going, it didn't look like it.

Murphy turned his horse to the trail, nudged him gently with his spurs, and held him in a lazy trot. A little rest wouldn't hurt the animal and he wanted some time to think. The small band of Apaches, mounted on unshod mustangs for the most part, had been traveling at a walk for the last three or four miles. They couldn't be too far ahead.

A few things had been nagging Al Murphy and he reflected on them. None of this Apache business made sense.

For the past several years the Mescaleros had been living peaceably on their mountain reservation near Fort Crosston. There had been no reports of unrest, and Murphy knew firsthand that the Indians were getting their full quota of beef. Christine McCormick had the contract to supply it from her ranch.

Most of the Mescaleros had taken up farming, and except for a severe alcohol and bootlegging problem that kept the major at the fort quite busy, the Apaches seemed content.

Then why this sudden, violent outbreak? Could it be that this band of renegades weren't Mescaleros?

It was possible, Murphy concluded. He'd learned in his Indian-fighting days that both the Chiricahuas and the Warm Springs Apache were more warlike than the Mescaleros. Chief Naiche and the medicine man Geronimo, along with their followers, had broken out of their reservation in Arizona months ago and were purportedly hiding in Mexico's Sierra Madre Mountains, making a living by raiding the local villages.

If one band of Apaches could break out, so could another. The Territory of New Mexico wasn't that far from Arizona.

The tracks stayed in the piñon-, cedar-, and juniper-studded fringe of the grassy plains to the north. Less than a mile ahead, the edge of the timber turned left, and Murphy wondered whether the Apaches would turn with it. If they did, it might mean that the Bar X ranch headquarters was their next target.

The tracks didn't turn. Instead, they headed straight east. If the renegades held their course, in a few miles they'd be in the harsh, forbidding badlands of the *malpais,* a prehistoric lava flow coating thousands of acres with a sharp, crusty, jumble of volcanic rock that made the land worthless and virtually impregnable.

Murphy wondered if the Indians knew where they were

headed and, if so, why they would go there. No one lived close to the *malpais,* and as far as he knew, there was no water. Could it be the Apaches knew they were being followed and were seeking a place of refuge, or more likely, a good place for an ambush?

The *grulla* slowed to a walk on his own and Murphy allowed it. While he wanted to stay close to the renegades, he didn't want to catch them until after dark, and he was probably closer to them now than he should be. Surprise was his only hope against such odds. If he could sneak up on their camp, in a matter of seconds the firepower of his double-action Smith and Wesson could cut their numbers in half.

But sneaking up on an Apache was a very difficult thing to do. In his experience, it usually worked the other way around.

Murphy reached down and touched the butt of his .40-60 Winchester, making sure it was still in the scabbard. It hadn't happened to him, but he knew of more than one man who'd reached for his rifle only to find it had slipped out of the scabbard miles behind.

The saddlebags behind the cantle that Murphy always kept ready for hurried emergencies like this one contained a four-day supply of jerky and hardtack, three pairs of handcuffs, a pair of army-issue binoculars, two boxes of 210-grain .40-60s, and two boxes of .44s for his pistol. With the additional ammunition in the loops of his cartridge belt, he figured he had enough for most anything.

Three miles farther down the gently sloped, brushy terrain and not too far from the edge of the *malpais,* the tracks entered a wide, deep, boulder-strewn canyon. Murphy followed on, warily scanning the sides and finding that the canyon continually narrowed as it dropped in elevation.

Murphy pulled the *grulla* up. He'd spent too much of his life chasing outlaws and Indians not to realize the danger he faced if he rode on. One man, carefuly hidden behind a rock, could easily kill him.

He looked up at the sun. The summer days were long and it was still a good hour and a half before dark. Without further deliberation, Murphy turned off the tracks and started the horse up the steep slope to his right. At the top, he should be able to watch the band's movements without being seen.

The horse's muscles tightened and bulged at the strenuous climb. Murphy grabbed a handful of mane with his right hand and leaned as far forward in the stirrups as possible to take his weight off the animal's kidneys and help him climb.

Halfway up the incline, a gunshot ripped through the quiet, echoing loudly in the canyon and ending all hope Murphy had for a surprise attack. He should have held the *grulla* back more, knowing he was getting too close to the renegades. Now things were going to be tough, and the role of who was after whom was becoming hard to distinguish.

A bullet kicked up dust a few yards behind Murphy and he hurriedly searched the far side of the canyon, able to see it much better than from the bottom. A barely visible puff of smoke revealed the sniper's location between two jagged shelves of rock.

Murphy judged the distance at over five hundred yards, much too far for any degree of accuracy with a Winchester or Henry. Nonetheless, there was always the chance the shooter could aim high and get lucky.

Murphy spurred the *grulla* hard. Another shot roared. He didn't look back. His attention was focused on a broad, egg-shaped boulder above him and the safety it would provide if he could reach it.

A third shot rang out as the *grulla* lunged behind the boulder and Murphy felt the big horse flinch, felt his left hindquarter drop, and knew the animal had been hit. He reached for his Winchester and leaped to the ground.

Blood oozed from a bullet hole two inches to the rear of the *grulla's* hipbone. Murphy hurriedly propped his rifle against the boulder and took out his handkerchief, ripping it in half. He stuffed part of it in the hole, then picked up a handful of dirt and further packed the wound to cake the blood and stop the bleeding. The bullet had to have lost a lot of power over the distance and if it hadn't hit a bone, the horse might be all right.

Two shots boomed, fired almost together, and a bullet ricocheted off the boulder. Murphy picked up his rifle, levered a shell into the barrel, and edged to the side for a look. The shots told him there were now two men shooting at him. Soon there'd be others.

An Indian darted between two rocks and Murphy threw his rifle to his shoulder and aimed, his rage almost causing him to empty the gun, though his years of fighting experience kept him from doing so. He'd only be wasting shells at that range, and it wouldn't hurt if his silence made the Apaches wonder what he was up to.

Reluctantly, Murphy let the hammer down on his rifle and moved back to the horse. The bleeding had almost stopped. He removed the saddle and wrapped one rein around the saddle horn to keep him from straying, then took his binoculars out of the saddlebags and stepped back to the edge of the boulder to keep watch on the Apaches' movements.

He knew he was in a tight spot and wondered for the first time if he'd taken on more than he could handle. Maybe he should have waited for Moses to get his horse and accompany him. Perhaps he should have deputized a posse. But it wasn't Murphy's way. Had never been his way.

Until coming to Turrett a year ago, Al Murphy had never had friends, not real friends like Skeet and Moses, who had risked their lives in the Turrett County war to help him.

But old habits die hard and Murphy had lived like a lone wolf too long to start running in a pack when he could help it. No one to depend on—or worry about—made the fighting easier, he believed.

The canyon was quiet. Nothing moved. Murphy tried to guess what the Apaches would do next. They, of course, knew he was alone, but they might think that others were sure to be on their way, and that could cause them to lose interest in him and flee.

Crazy as it seemed in his precarious position, Murphy didn't want them leaving. The *grulla* was in no shape for a chase, and if the fight didn't happen here and now, it might never happen at all, and the Prices' murderers would go free.

Murphy retrieved his canteen and saddlebags and placed them over his shoulder. He reasoned that whether the Apaches intended to leave or were now busily working to surround and kill him, the best thing to do was the unexpected.

He'd do what he came here to do. He would attack, hopefully hitting one or two of them before dark. It should make the others angry enough with him that they'd wait out the night, confident of getting even with him in the morning.

CHAPTER 5

A STIFF BREEZE started to blow as Murphy crouched low and ran from the protection of the boulder toward a lone, gnarled mesquite. He slid to a stop under it, expecting to hear the report of a rifle or the whine of a bullet.

Surprisingly, it didn't come. He looked to the west between the mesquite branches at a line of dark clouds forming. Rain was coming, but Murphy had lived in the southwest too long to try to outguess a desert thunderstorm. They rarely hit where he thought they would.

He looked down in the canyon and searched the other side. Nothing.

Had the renegades left? A foolish question, Murphy knew. No human was more adept in the art of camouflage and stealth than the Apache. Twenty braves could be fifty yards below him and not give a clue of their presence.

The breeze gusted and a whirlwind formed across the canyon, raising dust and a few dry tumbleweeds high into the air. Something moved along with it on the ground, possibly a bush, a fox, a coyote—or an Apache.

Murphy saw a ravine forty yards to his right that he hadn't noticed before. He waited for another gust of wind, knowing it would help to hide his movements, then made a wild dash toward the gully, hoping he'd find it deep enough to provide him with cover on his way to the bottom of the canyon.

If he could get to the bottom, he should be right in the middle of the Apaches and close enough to shoot accurately at them on either side of the canyon.

The ravine was almost *too* deep. Having no choice but to

slide over the edge when he reached it, he fell several feet, landing hard on his back, his rifle held carefully above in his left hand.

The air had been knocked out of him. He lay still a moment, gasping, then rose to his feet and looked down the ravine. Suddenly, he realized the full extent of what he'd gotten himself into. If the Apaches had seen him go into the gully, the steep ravine he'd hope would provide cover for him would soon turn into a trap with no way out.

Cautiously, Murphy stepped down the wash. He shifted his saddlebags and canteen to his left shoulder and took out the Smith, blowing the dust off the hammer and cylinder. If he ran into trouble here, the shooting would be fast and close.

The wind whistled above him, covering the crunching sound his boots made on the gravelly wash floor, and the light of dusk was growing dimmer by the minute.

His pace quickened. The farther down the ravine he went, the deeper and narrower it became. A vague shadow appeared on a dirt wall ahead, just before the ravine made a turn.

Murphy stopped, his nerves and muscles tight with tension. The shadow could be caused by most anything, a bush or a large rock—unless it moved.

The shadow moved. The man who made it would be around the corner in seconds. Murphy stood stone still, afraid his steps would be too loud and that any movement he made would create a warning shadow of its own.

Murphy's breathing stopped and his thoughts raced. From where he stood, it didn't seem possible, but if the approaching renegade could be taken captive instead of killed, he might prove useful.

The time for thinking ended. A long-haired Apache dressed in trousers and a half-opened shirt appeared with a rifle in his hands. Murphy brought the Smith up, taking the time to carefully aim while the Indian swung his cumbersome rifle to his armpit.

Fire and smoke belched from the muzzle of the Smith and the report of the gun was deafening in the confines of the ravine. The Apache's leg flew out from under him and he fell hard.

Murphy ran to him, quickly placing the muzzle of the Smith against the back of the man's head and cocking the hammer. His breathing was loud and voice shaky. "I . . . I don't know if you can understand me, but if you don't take your hands off that rifle, I'm going to blow your head off."

The Indian released the rifle. Murphy took it and threw it a few feet away, then ripped the renegade's long knife and sheath from his waist and placed it through his belt. He laid his Winchester to the side, put his knee in the middle of the Apache's back, and groped in his saddlebags for a pair of handcuffs. In seconds the Indian's hands were tightly cuffed behind him.

Murphy grabbed the brave by the shoulder and rolled him over. The man looked to be in his thirties and had a long ugly scar running from his temple to his chin. His narrow nose and high cheeks showed more Spanish ancestry than Apache and his cruel-looking brown eyes were wild and defiant. He spit in Murphy's face.

Like the strike of a rattlesnake, Murphy backhanded him, drawing blood to one corner of his mouth. The emotions Murphy had felt at the Price homestead this morning quickly flooded through him now that he had someone to take his rage out on. He grabbed a handful of the renegade's hair, jerked his head up, and slapped him again. "I should kill you. If you give me any trouble, any trouble at all, I will."

He released the Indian and stood. Most reservation Apaches understood and spoke at least some English. Murphy wanted to question the renegade to see if he could find out who he was up against and the why of it all. Any information he could get might prove to be extremely helpful. But the shot he'd fired was bound to draw some of the others, and he was in a very bad spot for a fight.

Quickly, he put his saddlebags and canteen over his shoulder and placed his Winchester and the Apache's lever-action Henry in the crook of his left arm. He pulled the man to his feet by the hair of his head.

The renegade's leg was bleeding heavily, but he had his weight on it, showing that the bone wasn't broken. The bleeding would have to wait. They *had* to get moving.

A few steps and the Indian pulled back hard and fell. Murphy mercilessly yanked his hair, using such force that it threatened to break his neck. The man climbed shakily to his feet, convinced that Murphy would make his earlier threat good.

Murphy moved out in the faint light, keeping a tight grip on his captive's hair.

Lightning streaked the sky, accompanied by a loud clap of thunder; large drops of rain began to fall, stopped, then fell again, heavier than before. A new threat loomed. Murphy had seen what even brief thunderstorms could do to the area's numerous arroyos. In just minutes this ravine could be filled with rushing muddy water from which there was no escape.

Faster and faster Murphy went, moving into a jog. The renegade followed, offering no more resistance. Murphy could only guess that he, too, realized the seriousness of their predicament.

A cut in the bank appeared a few yards ahead, looking like a tall, dark, uninviting door. A foot of foamy water gushed out the bottom. Murphy took a chance and entered without hesitation. The cut proved to be a side draw that offered a way out—if they could climb its muddy, slick, rain-filled base.

Murphy shoved the Indian in front of him and released

his hair. He gestured up the draw. "You first. If you try and run at the top, you'll get a bullet in the back."

The Apache started to climb and Murphy stayed close behind. He had no faith in his warning. The man would run and Murphy's only chance to stop him without killing him was to stay close.

Twice the renegade slipped and started to fall backward, not having the benefit of his hands to help him keep his balance. Both times Murphy caught him and pushed him on. An abrupt three-foot ledge was at the top and on reaching it, the brave thrust his body over and wildly scrambled to get his feet under him.

Murphy caught an ankle. The Indian kicked back with his other foot and Murphy had no choice but to drop the two rifles in his left arm and grab the kicking foot, pulling himself up and over his prisoner.

He landed a savage blow to the side of the renegade's head, knocking him unconscious.

The rifles. Murphy slid back into the draw and felt around in the muddy runoff until he found the two long guns. He laid them over the edge, then climbed out and lay facedown, exhausted and barely able to see his prisoner through the dark and pouring rain.

Murphy lay there several minutes, catching his breath and letting the tension inside him ease. At last he raised up and crawled to the Apache. The bleeding leg had to be tended to.

The heavy rain and darkness made the task difficult. Murphy took the renegade's knife from his waist and used it to slit open the pants leg. He felt above the knee on both sides of the leg, finding that the bullet had gone clean through, barely missing the bone.

He ripped a long, wide piece of cloth from the pants and tied a tourniquet above the wound, adjusting it tight enough that it would stop the bleeding yet allow circulation to the leg. He wondered how long the renegade would remain unconscious. Depending on the amount of blood he'd lost, he might never wake up.

The rain stopped as suddenly as it had come. Murphy looked up at the western sky, seeing several bright stars. A loud roar came from the river of gushing water that was flooding the ravine behind them. They'd been lucky to find a way out.

Murphy studied his situation. First and foremost, he needed a horse. By now the Apaches probably realized one of their number was missing. Whether that would be enough to hold them here, as Murphy had hoped, remained to be seen, and a man without a horse in this wide, open territory was terribly handicapped.

It was doubtful that the wounded *grulla* could carry Murphy far, if at all. And it was likely the Apaches had already killed or stolen the animal. Even if they hadn't, there was a good chance a few of them were stationed around the horse, waiting for Murphy to return for him. No, whatever the case, he needed a horse and the renegades were the only ones around who had any.

Another thought struck Murphy: the two hindquarters of beef the Indians had removed from the milk cow at the Price ranch—they wouldn't have taken the meat unless they were hungry and needed it. By tomorrow, it would spoil unless they ate or jerked it tonight, and for that, they'd need a fire.

Reminded of his own empty stomach, Murphy opened his saddlebags. He'd eat and wait, giving the Apaches time to congregate and build a fire, which he thought they would do if they'd decided to hang around until dawn to finish him off.

The presence of one white man in the area wasn't apt to cause them too much concern. If things went right, Murphy considered, he might get more than a horse.

A whole lot more.

CHAPTER 6

THE CAPTIVE RENEGADE woke up a little over an hour later. Murphy still wanted to question him, but was afraid their voices might alert any nearby Apaches of their location. He gagged the Indian, then bound his ankles tightly together with his belt and pulled him into the muddy side draw. The other Indians shouldn't be able to find him until daylight, and by then, Murphy would be back.

Murphy hid his canteen and his prisoner's Henry under a greasewood bush and picked up his saddlebags and the Winchester. While waiting, he'd cleaned the two rifles and his revolver as best he could. The guns were ready.

The night was black except for the faint starlight. Murphy moved out slowly, stepping carefully and quietly. In the darkness, it would be easy to step on a rattlesnake or fall into a hole—or run into an Apache.

Some folks believed Apaches wouldn't fight at night, but Murphy knew better. While it was true that many Indians shared the belief that "he who kills at night must walk in the darkness through the Place of Dead," there were others who did not, and it was a foolish man who would bet his life on the difference.

Murphy angled up the side of the canyon wall. The higher he got, the better were his chances of spotting the band's fire, if his reasoning about the cooking of the beef was correct.

He was almost to the top when he glimpsed it. He stopped, took a step back, and there was the tiny light again, maybe three-quarters of a mile away in the bottom of the canyon and close, he guessed, to the edge of the *malpais.*

Using even more caution than before, Murphy started toward it. He had plenty of time: it would be best if he didn't reach the camp until sometime after midnight. By then, the renegades would be lulled into a false sense of security and he'd have the element of surprise he so desperately needed.

As he walked, the horse he needed became secondary in his thoughts. Over and over the earlier scene inside the Prices' home flashed through his mind and with it came fierce anger directed at the murderers.

He realized that if he tried to steal a horse before attacking the camp and anything went wrong, he might lose both the horse and the renegades. That was a chance he didn't want to take.

At last, hours later, he sensed he was getting close, though it had been a while since he'd seen the light of their fire.

There were sure to be guards posted, at least one by their horses and a couple of others around the camp. It would be extremely difficult to try to sneak up on one of them. The best way, the only way, was to approach the camp from a direction that wasn't expected, and hopefully unguarded.

Murphy decided to cross the bottom of the canyon and climb halfway up the other side, then move below the camp and approach it from the *malpais.* It would take him a few more hours of nerve-wrecking, tiresome travel, but the Apaches wouldn't be expecting trouble from that direction.

A half-moon unexpectedly tipped over the canyon ridge to the east and Murphy was glad of it. His eyes had grown accustomed to the dark and he could see surprisingly well, but the additional light would make his task easier.

Some time later, Murphy stood watching the remaining

glowing embers of the Indian's campfire, which looked like so many eyes, staring at him.

A horse whinnied off to his left and Murphy realized he'd been fortunate. The horses could have been tethered between him and the camp, making it almost impossible to get past them without their alerting the Apaches of his presence.

A foot at a time Murphy crept forward, his saddlebags and Winchester in his left hand and the Smith in his right. Thirty yards farther, he could see several dark shapes on the ground that were the bodies of sleeping men.

He almost stopped, knowing he was close enough to do a lot of damage, then changed his mind and crept on. The closer he was, the deadlier he'd be. If they allowed it, he'd get right in the middle of them.

Too late he felt the unfamiliar shape of a piece of mesquite beneath his left boot. The large, dry stick snapped loudly. A man to the right jerked up from his bed and Murphy instinctively aimed and pulled the trigger on the double-action revolver, the blast ripping the night apart.

The man went down, sliding, and in a flash Murphy fell to his knees, releasing his grip on the Winchester and saddlebags and taking the Smith in both of his hands. The renegades jumped from their beds at a run, not even attempting to fight back.

Again and again Murphy pulled the trigger and the heavy revolver pounded his hands. The speed of his shots created a continuous, thundering roar.

Two more men fell, landing on the ground in a heap. A third shadow to the left of the fire leaped high into the air and let out a shrill cry.

Then, except for the rolling echo of the shots up the canyon, it was over. Nothing in view moved. Murphy holstered the empty Smith, grabbed his Winchester and saddlebags, and ran toward the sound of the horse he'd heard earlier. He didn't need to think. So far, everything had gone according to plan and he knew what came next.

In the confusion created by his attack, he hoped that any Apache who might see him going for the horses would be afraid to shoot for fear he was one of their own.

The outline of two horses appeared ahead. Murphy slowed to a walk, not wanting to spook the animals. He wasn't far from them when he heard the twang of a bowstring and the swish of an arrow. The arrow hit him solidly in the shoulder blade, knocking him down and causing him to lose his grip on the Winchester and saddlebags.

Quickly he regained his feet and broke into a wild, desperate run. The time it would take to retrieve the gun and bags wasn't worth the risk of taking another arrow—or perhaps a slug.

The two hobbled horses jumped away from him and he passed them by, going for the safety distance and darkness would provide.

A shot rang out behind him, accompanied by piercing yells. Murphy ran on. His shoulder was hit hard and bleeding heavily. He'd lost his rifle, his supply of ammunition, and his food.

Now he had to work to keep from losing his life.

CHAPTER 7

MURPHY STOPPED TO rest, leaning against a boulder. His lungs felt as if they were on fire and his muscles trembled in weakness. Excruciating pain from his arrow wound shot through him at his every move.

Gritting his teeth, he removed the Smith from his holster and began to load it with shells from his cartridge belt, at the same time trying to listen above his loud breathing for anyone approaching. The gun loaded, he replaced it, and reached over his back with his right hand to feel the shaft of the arrow.

He could only touch it with his fingers. There was nothing to be done, he realized. The arrowhead was solidly embedded in the bone of his shoulder, and to try to remove it would only make the bleeding worse.

In minutes his breathing eased somewhat and he walked on, moving slowly. The moon that had earlier helped him see his targets now threatened to help the Apaches find theirs.

An hour passed. Murphy guessed that the Apaches knew he was hit and had decided to wait for dawn to hunt him. Although events had turned against him, the night's work had not been a waste and Murphy took some comfort in that fact.

Counting his captives, at least five of the renegades were dead or wounded, almost half their number. A man, Murphy reassured himself, had no right to expect more than he'd accomplished.

Later, as the coming dawn started to erase the stars from the sky, Murphy stumbled wearily to the ground beside the bush he'd hid his canteen and the Henry under. Unable to rise again, he crawled and wormed his way into the side draw where he'd left his prisoner.

The Indian lay there, his eyes open and the gag still in his mouth. After glancing at him, Murphy ignored him and positioned himself so that he could see above the edge of the dirt embankment. The angry Apaches were sure to be coming soon.

Murphy drank long from his canteen, his loss of blood and the night's activities making him very thirsty. It was all he could do to hold his red, tired eyes open and he splashed a little of the water in his face. The pain in his shoulder had changed from a series of sharp, intense pangs brought on by his movements to a steady, almost unbearable, grinding ache.

The dawn light grew and Murphy wondered what the new day would bring. He had enough shells in his cartridge belt to load the cylinder in the Smith one more time and the magazine in the renegade's Henry was full, fortunately using the same .44 loads as his revolver. The Apaches weren't going to have an easy time of it.

But whether they got him or not, Murphy realized, he was· as good as dead. Without a horse, he couldn't reach help and the arrow wound would soon kill him.

The handcuffed renegade rolled to his side, drawing Murphy's attention. Murphy looked at him a moment, an idea suddenly forming. It might work, he decided. If not, he had nothing to lose.

With cold sweat beading his forehead, Murphy inched his way to the renegade's feet and cut the belt binding them together. He placed the long knife against the man's throat and removed the gag.

"I know you can understand me. Give me your name."

The Apache didn't speak, hardly breathed.

Murphy moved the knife to the man's ear and started to cut. "Tell me or—"

"Kaetennae. My name is Kaetennae." Murphy stopped cutting and the man went on. "You will die for this. My brother will open up your belly for the crows."

Murphy moved the knife back to the Indian's throat. The unexpected additional information made his plan even better, *if* he hadn't already killed this man's brother. "Maybe so," Murphy's voice was almost a whisper, "but you won't live to see it." He grabbed Kaetennae's hair and pulled. "Move up to the edge."

Kaetennae crawled and pulled his way up to the ledge at the head of the draw. Murphy forced him over it, hanging on to his hair and keeping the knife at his throat.

Sweat streamed down Murphy's face from the exertion, and for a moment he thought he would pass out. The light-headed, dizzy feeling passed. Murphy looked up at the side of the canyon. The sun would peek over the rim in minutes.

He waited a moment to catch his breath and gather his strength, then yelled, "Kaetennae is with me." He waited for the echoes to end. "I'll trade him for a horse . . . or cut his throat . . . It's up to you."

Silence. Nothing moved. Minutes passed that seemed hours. The sun tipped over the ridge, and in its glare Murphy squinted, barely able to see. Finally a loud, strong voice replied, "We will trade. We will bring you a horse."

Kaetennae started to speak, and Murphy changed the position of the knife so that the point pressed against the flesh under his chin.

Ten minutes later he heard the hollow sound of unshod hooves striking rock. The sun's glare was even worse than before, and it took some time before Murphy saw the two animals, led by a short, compact Apache. One of the horses had to be for Kaetennae, the other for Murphy.

Murphy wasn't a fool. He knew the renegades had no intention of making a fair trade. They intended to kill him, if they could.

Still, no other options were open to him if he wanted to live—and unlike a year ago when he rode into Turrett, he now had a lot to live for.

The horses and renegades came closer. Murphy wondered if he had the strength to carry out the rest of his plan. Before mounting, he would train the Smith on Kaetennae. Then he'd . . .

A shot boomed from somewhere behind, sounding more like a small cannon than a gun. Murphy turned his head and out of the corner of his eye saw an Apache fall by the ravine thirty yards away.

Murphy knew of only one gun around that made a horrendous noise like that. It was a Sharps .50-90 long-range buffalo rifle. A gun that was as big and powerful as the man who owned it. It was the only gun Moses Coffin owned.

The sound of running hooves came, and Murphy quickly let go of Kaetennae's hair and shifted the knife at the man's throat to his left hand. He pulled out his revolver and started to level it on the fleeing Apache, who now rode one of the horses while leading the other.

Moses' awesome-sounding rifle boomed again and Murphy saw his would-be target fly off the horse.

A few more shots came, fired by the Apaches from the canyon walls, then it was still.

Quiet.

Murphy pointed the muzzle of the Smith at Kaetennae, returning the long knife to his belt. If Moses was here, and he had to be, he'd come at just the right time. Murphy had been right about the Apaches. They had no intention of making a fair trade, but then, Murphy hadn't figured on holding up his end of the bargain either.

Soon Murphy heard the sound of a horse plodding slowly toward him. He looked down in the canyon and saw Moses on his huge buckskin workhorse, carrying the heavy

Sharps rifle ready across his lap. No sight in Murphy's memory had ever been more welcome.

The big man dismounted. "I see'd a bunch of them Apaches ridin' out over the top. I guess, if that be all of them, they's gone." Moses pointed to the other side of the canyon. "From over there, it surely did look like you was in trouble."

Murphy holstered the Smith. "Just a little." He managed a grin. "I don't know what you're doing here, but I'm sure glad you showed up."

"It was Miss Christine. When me and Skeet got back to town and told her everythin', she was real worried about you. She found another driver for the freight wagon and sent me along after you."

Murphy reached his hand out. "Help me out of here, will you?"

Moses took Murphy's hand and gently pulled him out of the narrow draw. "You sure do look bad. That arrow's got to come out." He pointed at Kaetennae. "He one of them what was at the Price place?"

Murphy nodded. Moses' eyes turned cold and his expression blank. He stepped beside Kaetennae and put the muzzle of the Sharps a few inches from the renegade's nose.

Then he pulled the hammer back.

"No, Moses. We need him. There's a lot we don't know yet."

Moses' hands shook. Kaetennae's wide eyes were glued to the shotgun-sized bore.

At last, Moses let the hammer down. He threw his floppy brown hat to the ground and glared at Murphy.

"You lied to me, sayin' this was a military matter and that all you was gonna do was follow along. I shoulda let 'em kill you. When you gonna learn that two mens can fight better than one?

"If you'da let me come, maybe you wouldn't be hurtin'

so much right now and maybe them murderin' Apaches that just run over the hill wouldn't be gettin' away."

Murphy looked down like a scolded child. He knew he had it coming. "You're right, but I did get a few of them last night." Then he told Moses to do something he knew full well he wouldn't. "You go on after them. I'll be all right."

Moses stepped closer to Murphy. "I ought to leave you. You get on over on your belly and let me see if I can get that arrow out."

Murphy half fell from his knees, his arms too weak to hold his weight. He groaned. "Keep . . . keep an eye on that renegade. His leg's hurt, but he might try and run."

Moses patted the stock of his heavy Sharps. "I wish he would."

Arrow wounds were something Moses knew about. He'd seen a lot of them during his army days, two of them his own. He tore the shirt around the wound and pulled out his knife. "This gonna hurt some."

"Wait," Murphy said. "I . . . I may pass out. The *grulla,* I left him on the ridge above us by a boulder. He's hit."

"I'll be goin' to look for him when we's done."

The hunting knife was razor sharp and Moses cut the purplish flesh around the shaft, dilating the hole and allowing him to feel the back of the arrowhead. Murphy lay still, his fists clenched so tight they were white.

"You is one lucky man, Al. They ain't no barbs on the arrowhead like they is on a war arrow. This is a huntin' arrow. Gone deep in the bone though."

Moses straddled Murphy and took the shaft in both hands. He had to pull straight and hope the sinew holding the arrowhead to the shaft didn't break.

He pulled up, gently at first, then increasing the pressure. Murphy gasped and moaned, his body trembled. Moses pulled harder. The shaft came out and Murphy jerked up against the pain, then flopped back to the ground, unconscious.

Moses examined the end of the shaft. The flint arrowhead wasn't on it. He broke the arrow in disgust and threw it. He had no pliers. Doc Woods would have to fish the head out later.

After bandaging the wound as best he could and securely tying up Kaetennae with his lariat, Moses went to hunt for the *grulla*. He returned over an hour later, rolled Murphy over, and spilled a little water from his canteen onto Murphy's face.

Murphy woke, wiping at the water. "Did . . . did you get it?"

"Naw. The head still be in there. Better get you on back to town."

"The *grulla*?"

Moses hesitated. He knew how much Murphy thought of the horse. "I found him. They done cut his throat and butchered the back straps off him."

Murphy closed his eyes. He had guessed it, somehow even known it. The Apaches would have taken the horse if he'd been able to go. The hip wound must have been worse than Murphy had thought. Things wouldn't be the same without the horse. Murphy had owned him a long time.

Moses pulled his buckskin up and Murphy shakily tried to get to his feet. Moses helped him rise and leaned him against the horse.

His voice was gruff. "That Apache ain't able to walk neither. He'll have to ride with you, 'less I kill him so's he won't be murderin' no more little babies."

Murphy looked at Kaetennae. The Apache's fierce eyes and expression showed no sign of fear.

"No. Untie him and give him some water. In town, when I'm able, we'll get what we can out of him and when the circuit judge comes, we'll hang him."

CHAPTER 8

AL MURPHY OPENED his eyes and blinked against the bright sunlight coming through a window. A hand gently touched his forehead and he turned over to see Christine McCormick at his side and Doc Woods at the foot of the bed. Christine took a damp washcloth and wiped his brow.

"Where . . . where . . ." As he started to ask the question, the answer came to him. He was in Christine's room at the Mercantile. She stayed in town more than she did at the ranch, and part of the back of the store had been partitioned off into two rooms, giving her a small kitchen and a bedroom.

Christine's voice was soft. "You're here at the store. Moses brought you in late last night."

It was a moment before the events of the preceding day became organized in Murphy's mind. "I must've went out. The Apache . . . my prisoner, is . . ."

Doc Woods interrupted. "He's at my office. Moses is with him. I had to take his leg off. Gangrene had set in, but he'll be fine."

The doctor shifted the stub of a cigar from one corner of his mouth to the other. "I took that arrowhead out of your back. You'll be sore and weak for a few days. You lost a good bit of blood."

Murphy tried to raise up, and pain shot through his shoulder. Christine put her hand behind his head and eased him down. "You lay still. I'm disgusted enough with you as it is. I suppose you think you're invincible. One man, going after an entire band of Apaches. It's idiotic. If Moses hadn't found you, you'd be dead."

A thin smile formed on Murphy's lips. "I had a plan."

"Moses told me about it. It didn't look to him like your plan was working."

Murphy didn't reply. Christine rinsed the washcloth out in a bowl beside the bed and wiped his face, more roughly than before.

The doctor moved to the door. "I'll be back this afternoon to change your bandages." He smiled. "Looks like I'm leaving you in good hands. Better try to get him to eat something, Christine."

"Wait, Doc," Murphy said. "How's Travis?"

The doctor hesitated, then stepped beside Christine. "He's dead. Someone broke into my house last night and killed him."

Murphy started to get up again, but Christine held his chest down. Travis Price, who was barely alive, had been murdered? It was incomprehensible.

"Did you see anything?"

"Yes and no. A noise woke me and I lay there, thinking it was probably just the wind. A moment later I was sure I heard footsteps on my squeaky wood floor.

"I lit a lamp and went into the room where Travis was, finding the curtains blowing in the breeze. Knowing I'd shut all the windows, I went to it and saw the outline, really only a blur, of a man running away. Except that he wore a hat, I couldn't tell you another thing about him."

"What kind of hat?"

"I don't know, it was too dark. Just a hat, maybe the high-crowned type some of the cowboys around here wear."

"How did he kill Travis?"

"He stabbed him, once in the heart and once close to it."

"Think, Doc. Did Travis ever say anything? Is there anything else? The smallest detail might be helpful."

The doctor shook his head. "Sorry. He never spoke. There's nothing else." He started for the door. "I better get on back and check on that Indian you and Moses brought in. You just rest."

"Thanks, Doc."

The door closed. Christine stood. "I'll get you something to eat."

She left the room and Murphy pondered the latest twist of events. Obviously, someone wanted Travis dead, so much so that when the band of Apaches failed to kill him, he did it himself, or had it done.

But why? What threat could Price have been to anyone? Was it possible that all of Murphy's thinking about the attack on the Price homestead had been wrong? That it wasn't haphazard at all, but a shrewdly and carefully planned assault?

Or was he wrong again? Could the two attacks be unrelated and simply coincidental? No, that idea seemed improbable. The events were too close together and were both aimed at the same person. But why was the entire family killed? Surely Mrs. Price and her girls hadn't harmed anyone. What kind of a man, or men, would want a pregnant woman and her two small children dead?

There were no answers to his many questions, but one thing was clear to Al Murphy. Travis Price had to have been murdered because of something he'd done, might do, or knew. If the attack by the Apaches was in fact a part of some kind of scheme, Kaetennae might be next. Depending on what the renegade knew, whoever was behind all of this couldn't take a chance on him talking.

Murphy squirmed sideways to the edge of the bed, let his feet fall to the floor, and braced himself for the pain he knew would come when he raised himself up.

He'd just made it to a sitting position when Christine stepped into the room, almost dropping the bowl of stew at the sight of him. She angrily set the stew on her dresser, spilling some of it, and looked at Murphy's flushed, sweaty face.

"What are you doing? Didn't you hear the doctor? He said you'd lost a lot of blood and needed to rest." She pointed her finger. "Look at you. You're so weak you barely made it up. How far do you think you'll get before you fall and I have to find help to get you back in bed?"

Murphy was about to speak when Christine stomped over to him and started to force him back down.

"No. Wait." She stopped pushing and he continued, "I've got to go. I think Kaetennae . . . ah . . . the Apache we brought in, he may be killed. There—there may be a whole lot more to all of this than we know, and I haven't had a chance to question him. I need to get him in jail for safekeeping and find out what he knows."

"What you need to do, Mr. Murphy, is lie down and rest."

She laid him back, finding from his lack of resistance that he was even weaker than she'd believed.

"Moses will guard the Indian. If he's able and the doctor allows it, we'll put him in the jail. After that, I'll tell Moses you want him to try and find out what he can from the man, right after"—she gently swung his legs onto the bed—"you eat and go to sleep."

Murphy watched her go for the bowl on the dresser, realizing he was a lucky man. Christine McCormick wasn't just pretty, she was smart, and he trusted her completely. She'd handle things until he was able, then he'd tend to them himself. From the looks of things, he was going to have his hands full.

CHAPTER 9

A HEAVY KNOCK on the outside door of Christine's quarters roused Murphy from his half-sleep. Since yesterday, and for the last twenty-four hours, he'd been resting. After feeding him breakfast earlier, Christine had left to go up front and help out in the store.

"Come in," Murphy called, surprised at the strength in his voice. He glanced at his gun belt hanging on the bedpost and started to reach for the Smith, then changed his mind. An enemy wouldn't be knocking.

Moses lowered his head to get through the open bedroom door.

"Hello, Moses." Murphy smiled.

The big man stopped at the foot of the bed. "Howdy, Al. I just be comin' by to check on you. You be lookin' fine."

"I am, Moses. I'll be up and around in another day or two. Probably could now, but you know how Christine and the Doc are."

"You just rest and do what they tell you. Everythin' be just fine."

Murphy carefully propped himself up against the headboard. He felt much better, except his shoulder was still awfully sore. "Christine told me you put Kaetennae in jail. How is he?"

"He be all right, 'cept he's weak. I tried to get him to talk like Miss Christine said you wanted me to, but he won't say nothin'. He just looks at me with them mean, wild-lookin' eyes of his."

"Did you threaten him, try to make him talk?"

"I did do it. I told him we was gonna hang him. Told

44

him if he told us everythin', it might go better for him. It didn't change him none. I ain't sure he knows what I be sayin'."

"He understands," Murphy said. "Don't worry about it. Tomorrow or the next day I'll try and talk to him. Is someone with him?"

Moses nodded. "The doc. He done finished bandaging him and said he would stay there a few minutes if I wanted to come see you."

"You better get back, then. Thanks for staying with him."

"Ain't much trouble." Moses took a step, then stopped. "What we gonna do about them Apaches what got away? Ain't right that they go free after what they done. Me and some of the men here in town could go after 'em.

"No, not yet."

Murphy had spent much time thinking and decided that if his latest ideas were correct and the raid on the Price ranch was part of something bigger, the Apaches might return to their reservation without causing any further trouble.

Not that he didn't intend to go after them and try to see that they paid for what they'd done, but that could wait. If things worked out right, he might not have to.

"I need you here," Murphy continued, "at least until I get on my feet. Skeet should have reached Fort Crosston yesterday and told the major what happened to the Prices. Troops are bound to be on their way, and we'll let them spend their time hunting down the renegades."

Murphy scratched under the sling on his left arm. "Between trying to find out who killed Travis at Doc's and looking after Kaetennae, we've got enough to keep us busy for a while right here in Turrett."

Moses waited a moment before speaking. "Guess you be right. Don't any of it make no sense. Hope them soldiers shows up soon or them Apaches'll be clean out of the country. Well, I be seein' you."

"Thanks for coming by, Moses, both times."

Moses grinned and walked out the door. At noon, Christine returned.

"I brought you some company," she said.

Her sister-in-law smiled. Sarah was a petite, shy woman with jet-black hair, brown eyes, and a finely cut, thin face. In her own way, she was quite pretty. Billy, who was small for his age and looked a lot like her, approached the bed with his hand out.

"Howdy, Sheriff."

Murphy shook the boy's hand. Several times in the last few months he and Billy had gone riding together at the ranch and they'd become friends.

"Did you get them outlaws?" Billy asked.

Murphy smiled. "A few of them, deputy. I would have got 'em all, but I was waiting for you to come and help."

Billy looked down with a somber expression, obviously thinking. Seconds later his face brightened. "I was on my way, but my horse started limping. I had to turn back home."

Christine and Sarah covered their mouths, trying to keep from laughing. They had listened to Murphy and Deputy Billy talk about their daring exploits before and it never failed to amuse them.

"I knew it," Murphy replied, a twinkle in his eye. "I knew something had happened. You're my best deputy. You'd have been right there with me if you could have."

Billy nodded. Sarah moved beside her son, putting her arm around his shoulders. She liked Murphy and whenever he was out at the ranch, she cooked a big meal and made a special effort to show he was welcome.

"I'm glad you are doing well," Sarah said. "If I know you"—she glanced at Christine—"you won't be in this bed very long."

Christine stepped up, her voice sharp. "Yes, he will. At least another week."

Murphy and Sarah smiled as she took Billy by the hand. "I'm glad we came, but we'd better go. I bought some cheese and a few other things that will ruin in this heat if we don't get them home."

At the door, Murphy stopped them. "Deputy?"

Billy turned around.

"I'll be seeing you soon. There's a bunch of bad outlaws out there and we've got to figure out how we're going to bring them in."

"Sure thing, Sheriff. My . . . my horse, he's better. I can ride him now."

Sarah and Billy left. Christine pulled the blanket off the bed and folded it neatly, leaving Murphy with the sheet over him. "I'm going into the kitchen and fix us some lunch. The doctor should be here soon to change your bandages."

"I'm not very hungry, but I'd sure like a smoke."

Christine stepped out of the room. In a moment she returned, standing in the doorway with his tobacco sack. "You can have it, right after you eat."

She dropped the sack in the pocket of her white store apron and went into the kitchen.

CHAPTER 10

MURPHY LAY IN the dark bedroom, unable to sleep, listening to the music from a piano being played in the saloon across the street from the store. It seemed that in the last thirty minutes or so, the noise of the crowd inside had become increasingly louder, drowning out many of the notes.

He guessed the time at close to midnight, which provided a reason for the commotion. The men at the bar had been drinking for hours and the effect of the whiskey was starting to show.

Shouts came, yells that were too loud to be coming from inside the saloon. Murphy threw the covers back and slowly got out of bed, careful not to move or bump his left shoulder.

His legs felt strong beneath him, and he quietly stepped to the window and opened it. Several men were gathered in the street, a few holding torches and lanterns.

One man stepped out from the rest, a rope held high above his head. "What are we waitin' for? One man can't stop us. Let's get him!"

Murphy quickly turned from the window, forgetting about his wound. The sudden move caused a bolt of pain in his shoulder blade, and he waited a second for it to pass before moving to the bed and reaching for his gun belt.

The room brightened and Murphy turned to see Christine step through the doorway wearing a long nightgown and holding a lamp. Since Murphy's coming, she'd been sleeping on a cot in the kitchen.

"What are you doing?"

"My pants, my boots, where are they? A lynching party's outside. They're drunk and they're going for the jail."

Christine hesitated only briefly. The edge in Murphy's voice told her that she wasn't going to be able to stop him. He'd leave barefoot and in his long underwear if he had to, and maybe he did have to. Moses was at the jail alone.

"I'll get them," she said quietly. She quickly returned from the kitchen and helped him put his pants on and slide his bare feet into his boots. With his left arm in the sling, he was having difficulty tying down the holster around his leg and she helped him with that too. Then she followed him into the kitchen and opened the door for him.

"Be careful."

Murphy left without replying, walking as quickly as his sore back and shoulder would allow. His thoughts were on another day, a day he'd never been able to forget though he'd tried to put it behind him.

He was sheriff then too. Sheriff of Fletcher, Wyoming, a town filled with fools. And that day he hadn't been able to stop the lynching.

A boy, maybe seventeen years old, had lost his life at the end of a rope—for nothing. He hadn't done anything wrong. A young cowboy in a saloon managed to badger him into a fight and when the gun smoke cleared, the kid was still standing.

Someone said the cowboy who had been killed was the only son of local people, and that he'd been gunned down in cold blood. It wasn't true. Both young men had ridden into town with a herd, and the fight had been a fair one.

But the fools in Fletcher wouldn't listen, couldn't stand the thought of "one of their own" being murdered. They hit Murphy with a pick handle from behind, took the boy, and hanged him.

Murphy watched helplessly, watched the boy kick and scream and gag until death finally ended his suffering.

And in that moment, Murphy swore it would never happen again.

Swore that as long as there was breath in him, no other town would ever take a prisoner away from him, whether that prisoner needed hanging or not.

The crowd in front of the small, rock jail had grown to fifteen men. Some were talking loudly among themselves, others were yelling. Murphy crossed the street and came up behind and to the side of them.

Moses was on the porch, holding the Sharps buffalo gun across his arms. He was a powerful man and a good fighter, but the mob was more than he could handle, Murphy thought. The crowd would take advantage of his usual good nature, knowing he wasn't likely to shoot.

No one noticed as Murphy continued to move, working to get beside Moses. He was only a few feet away when the leaders of the group rushed the big man.

Murphy reached for the Smith, at the same time hearing a heavy thud and a man cry out. He held the revolver high above his head and started to pull the trigger when he saw two men thrown into the others like heavy sacks of grain.

He hesitated a second longer. Maybe he'd been wrong. Maybe Moses could handle this bunch, all fifteen of them.

The flash of a rifle barrel appeared in the light of a torch, and Murphy pulled the trigger on the Smith, sending a bullet into the air. The fight had to be stopped. Moses' brawn was no match for bullets. He fired the pistol again and it was quiet. No one moved.

Cautiously, Murphy stepped onto the boardwalk in front of the jail, careful to keep his back against the wall. This wasn't going to be a repeat of what happened in Wyoming. If they got him, they'd have to do it from the front.

"It's me, Moses. Al. Train your rifle on that man in front of you. If he moves, kill him. I mean it."

Moses took a step back against the jail door and the hammer on his Sharps clicked loudly.

"You can't get us all, Sheriff. The Prices were our friends and neighbors. That Indian in there's going to hang. We're going to see to it."

Murphy couldn't tell for sure who was speaking. "Move up slowly," he said. "I want to see who you are."

A short man appeared and Murphy recognized him instantly. He was Clyde Harrelson, owner of the Bar X ranch and the man who had killed Ben Simson months ago.

Murphy held the Smith on him. "You're not going to do anything, Clyde." He shifted his eyes to the mob. "None of you are going to do anything. You all know me. You know I'll use this gun if you push me.

"Now I want you all to go on home. When the circuit judge comes to town, there'll be a trial. No hanging is going to take place until then."

A murmur spread among the group, and a few of the men started to walk away. Clyde turned his head, seeing them.

"Wait! It might be months before the judge comes. You can see that the sheriff here is an Indian lover. He's protectin' that murderin' butcher inside. He's bluffing. There's too many of us and he knows it."

Murphy's mind was made up. In Fletcher, he'd hesitated to use his gun on the town citizens and he'd had to live with the consequences ever since. Kaetennae deserved to die. No one knew that any better than Murphy. But it wasn't going to happen like this.

"You're first, Clyde. I'm tired of talking. I'm going to kill you first."

A shivering sensation traveled the length of Clyde's spine. Never had he heard a voice so cool, so sure and deadly. He'd been wrong. Murphy would kill him, he was certain of it.

Slowly he raised both hands. "You—you win. If that Indian means so much to you that you'd shoot law-abiding honest men to protect him, then so be it. But this ain't over. We'll be back. You can bet on it."

Murphy's grave expression didn't change. "I'll be waiting."

Clyde turned and angrily shoved his way to the outside of the group. "Come on, boys. I'm buyin'. There'll be another time."

Murphy and Moses watched the crowd move down the street toward the saloon. Murphy wasn't too rattled by Harrelson's threat. The man was drunk. They were all drunk and he really couldn't blame them. The brutal murder of the entire Price family wasn't an easy thing to take. He was just glad Clyde hadn't forced him to use his gun.

He put the revolver in his holster. Moses pointed across the street. "Look, Miss Christine be comin'."

Christine appeared out of the shadows wearing a shawl over her nightgown and carrying a rifle. She came closer.

"You've been over there the whole time, haven't you?" Murphy asked.

She stepped up on the porch between the two men. "I thought you might need help. I should have known you didn't."

Murphy tried to keep from smiling. He wanted to be angry with her but couldn't. If things had gone badly, she might have been hurt. He couldn't stop his smile any longer. "I might've." He put his good arm around her waist. "And you'd be the best-looking help I ever had."

Moses opened the door to the jail and the three went in. Kaetennae watched them from a corner, where he sat on a blanket, resting against the rock wall. Murphy stepped to the iron bars. Except for the bloody bandage on the short stump of his right leg, the renegade looked well.

"They were going to hang you." Murphy took a chance on his earlier thoughts. "But there's others that want to kill you because they're afraid you'll talk. If you help me, tell me where you're from and why you and your brother murdered the Prices, I'll see that you stay alive a while longer."

The Apache lifted the end of the bloody stump with his right hand. His eyes and expression were fierce and hateful looking. "You did this. Kill me. Do it now! I do not care."

Murphy stared at him a little longer, then turned and went to his desk, certain that further talk was pointless. The Indian flat didn't care, and Murphy knew firsthand it was impossible to deal with a man like that. It wasn't so long ago that he'd been the same way.

He opened the bottom drawer and took out a whiskey bottle. For the last few days he'd had a terrific craving for a drink, the same craving that had almost destroyed him before coming to Turrett.

The bottle was half full and had been in the drawer for at least a month. He had been careful with it, and he'd be careful now. One drink, that's all, a big one.

He handed the bottle to Moses. "You first. I wouldn't have butted in out there, but I was afraid you were going to beat those boys to death."

Moses grinned, took a drink, and handed the bottle back. Murphy eased himself into the desk chair. "Christine? I've got a glass."

She shook her head. "No, you get your drink and then you're going back to the store to rest."

Murphy took a long pull, corked the bottle, and put it back into the drawer. He waited a moment for the alcohol to quit burning.

"I'm going to be all right. My strength's beginning to come back. I appreciate all that you've done, but I better stay here. I still think someone may try and kill him." He gestured at Kaetennae.

Christine's green eyes widened. "They just did, didn't they?"

"Yeah," Murphy muttered, suddenly wondering why he hadn't questioned it before. Was it possible that there was more to the lynch mob than a bunch of drunks seeking revenge?

It was something to think about.

CHAPTER 11

FOR OVER AN hour, Al Murphy had searched the area around Doc Woods's home for anything that might help lead him to Travis Price's murderer. He found a few boot prints, none of which were clear enough to do him any good, and nothing else, not even a horse track.

Finally giving up, Murphy stepped into the dusty street, looking east. The troops from Fort Crosston should have already come. Skeet, driving a slow freight wagon, was due back this evening. Something had to be wrong.

Murphy gazed a moment longer, then walked up the street toward the jail. Two days had passed since the night of the lynch party, and other than the soreness in his shoulder blade, he felt good. The sling on his left arm was only there to hold down his movements. He didn't think he needed it.

Moses sat inside the jail, by the small, potbellied stove, meticulously cleaning his Sharps. He looked up as Murphy walked in. "Did you find somethin'?"

Murphy sat down behind his desk. "No, not a thing."

"What you gonna do?"

Murphy leaned back and propped his feet up. "I wish I knew. When Skeet comes in, we'll see what he knows. If the military doesn't come, and it doesn't look like they're going to, I'll go out and try and pick up the Apaches' trail where we left it."

"I be goin' with you."

"You can't. Someone's got to stay here."

Moses set the Sharps against the wall and stood, a scowl on his face. "That arrow in you didn't learn you nothin', did it? They ain't no more freight runs for a week. Skeet can stay here. I be goin'."

Murphy grinned, wanting to soothe his friend's anger. It was apparent that Moses wasn't going to be talked out of going again. "I can see that you're going, and I'm glad of it. Two guns are better than one, right?"

Moses nodded and had started to sit back down when the front door opened and Christine walked in, holding a large basket in her hands. "I brought you both some lunch." She looked toward Kaetennae's cell, her expression sober. "There's enough here for him too."

Murphy stood and she set the basket on his desk. "Come outside with me. I want to show you something before you eat."

Christine led Murphy around the jail to the small corral he'd built for the *grulla*. A powerfully built, line-backed dun stood inside, sniffing at a fairly new saddle on the fence. The yellow-brown horse with black mane, tail, and socks backed away as they came closer. Murphy had seen the young horse before out at the ranch and had commented on his good looks.

"I know he can't replace the *grulla*," she said. "But you've said you thought he had a lot of potential. Some of the hands have ridden him with a hackamore and they say he's gentle, but he doesn't know much. He's yours, if you want him."

"Want him?!" Murphy held his hand out over the fence and the big colt moved haltingly to him, sniffing. "Of course I want him, but I can't take him. He's the best young stud you have and you were going to keep him to breed your mares, remember?"

Christine rested her arms on the top rail. "That was before you lost the *grulla*." She touched his arm. "I want you to have him. You need a good horse."

Murphy stepped through the corral rails. His face lit up

like a boy on his birthday. "Tell Moses to bring a rope and a hackamore. Might as well get started."

Christine laughed. "No, you don't. Your lunch is in the jail. You and Moses have plenty of time to work with him later."

After eating, Murphy rode the four-year-old colt most of the afternoon, happy for his wound's sake that the animal wasn't inclined to buck. The horse was smart, and Murphy firmly but patiently tuned his response to the pressure on the hackamore and the gentle nudging of his boot heels. It would be months, Murphy judged, before the dun was a polished riding horse, but in the meantime, he was green-broke enough to take Murphy wherever he needed to go.

At dark the two McCormick freight wagons arrived from Fort Crosston. Moses followed them to the store to help unhitch while Murphy waited at the jail, knowing that as much as Skeet liked to talk, he wouldn't, not until his mules were fed and watered. The small, wiry man took his work seriously and was considered one of the finest mule skinners in the country.

A half hour later, Skeet, Moses, and Christine walked into the lantern-lit jail. Murphy rose from his chair. "Where's the troops, Skeet? Why aren't they here?"

"They ain't comin'. Ain't nobody comin'." He moved to Kaetennae's cell. "I see you got one of 'em. Is he all you got? Why I coulda done better than that with my Greener, old as I am. You—"

"Skeet!" Murphy often lost patience with the little old man, who had a habit of using ten words when one would do.

Skeet turned his heavily wrinkled face toward Murphy. "What? No use in you hollerin' at me." He moved to Murphy's desk and opened the drawer holding the bottle.

"I'm tired and I want a drink to wash down the dust. It

ain't none of my fault that you cain't get but one of 'em. No need in you . . ."

Christine and Moses were smiling. Christine sat down on the edge of the desk and Moses took a chair by the stove, knowing that this was going to take a while. Skeet took a drink and held the bottle.

"Did you talk to Major Hilleary?" Murphy asked. "Did you tell him what happened at the Prices'?"

"Of course I did. Do you think I'm a dad-blamed idiot? Just 'cause I'm old don't mean I'm stupid."

"What did he say?"

"He ain't got nobody to come. They ain't more'n a dozen soldiers at the fort. Place looks plumb empty. Some big general ordered everybody out after Geronimo. He's down in Mexico, you know?"

Skeet noticed the sour look on Murphy's face. "Well, I guess you don't know. But he is, and everybody in the army's down there after him. They won't catch him though. That old Apache's like me. He ain't lived all these years for nothin'. Why I remember . . ."

Murphy took the bottle away from Skeet. "What else did he say? Did he know if any of the Mescalero braves had broken out of the reservation?"

"Naw, he don't . . ." Skeet stopped and fumbled at the top buttons of his shirt. "Dang it. I purt near forgot. The major, him and two more soldiers saddled up and left the fort soon as I told 'em what them Apaches done. 'Fore I left the next mornin', the major give me this." He took a letter out of his shirt. "He said for me to give it to you."

Murphy hurriedly opened the letter. He was acquainted with Major Hilleary, the commander of Fort Crosston, and believed him to be an intelligent, fair, and capable officer. During the Turrett County war, Murphy had killed two men at the post, men who were about to shoot Skeet and Moses.

The witnesses to the shooting lied about how it happened, and if it hadn't been for Major Hilleary's thorough investigation, Murphy would have been convicted of murder and executed or, at the least, sent to prison for life.

Murphy looked over the letter a moment, hesitant to read it out loud in Kaetennae's presence, then decided it didn't matter.

Sheriff Murphy,

I am deeply distraught over the apparent Apache outbreak in your area reported to me by Mr. Ames, and the subsequent wanton slaughter of an entire family thereof. Further, my heart is heavy with the knowledge that I am unable to provide you with immediate assistance. My command is committed for some time.

Through an extremely hasty personal inquiry and inspection of the Mescaleros near here, I have been able to determine that a number of young warriors are indeed missing, evidently having been lured off the reservation by the promise of large amounts of liquor and plunder by one Pionsenay Sanchez, a man of mixed Spanish descent whose large family is well known in this area for their acts of devilment and thievery. Whiskey-peddling to the Indians on the reservation has become an increasingly severe problem, and for some time now I have suspected the Sanchez brothers are involved, although I have no evidence to support this accusation.

Sanchez is approximately five feet nine inches tall, has long black hair, dresses like an Apache, and wears a large silver medallion around his neck.

Utilizing the resources available to me, I will remain on constant vigil should the renegades return, and send prompt notification at the occurrence of such act. I can only hope the above information will prove helpful and wish I were able to do more.

Please accept my sincere regrets. Your friend,

Major R. J. Hilleary.

Murphy carefully folded the letter. Skeet shook his head. "Gibberish, that's all it is. I don't see why that major ain't smart enough to talk like everybody else so's people can understand him. Nice-enough fellow though. Always treats me good."

Christine stood up and Murphy looked at her. He didn't think he'd told her, or Moses either, for that matter. He gestured at Kaetennae, who watched them from his usual position in the corner of the cell.

"Kaetennae told me in the canyon where we had the fight that he had a brother. He threatened me with him, and guessing from the Spanish look to Kaetennae, I'd say this Pionsenay Sanchez the major speaks of is him."

Murphy stepped to the cell door. "Is that right? Is Pionsenay Sanchez your brother?"

Kaetennae glared at Murphy, and to everyone's astonishment, he spoke. "He is my brother. I have many brothers. They will cut your heart out for this." He pointed to the stub of his leg. "They will come for me and you will die. You will all die!"

Murphy shook the cell door. "Why? Why did your brother promise the Apaches liquor and plunder if they'd go with him? What was his purpose? The family you butchered had no whiskey or much of anything else."

Kaetennae looked down without responding. It was all Murphy could do to keep from unlocking the cell and trying to beat the much-needed information out of the man, yet he knew it wouldn't help. The renegade, half-breed, or whatever he was had already shown that he wouldn't talk unless he chose to do so.

Christine stepped beside Murphy. "At least you know more than you did. You have a name."

"Yeah," Murphy answered, his eyes on Kaetennae. "I guess that's a start."

CHAPTER 12

SKEET, MOSES, AND Christine left the jail, leaving Murphy to puzzle over the latest developments. The fact that the renegades were definitely Mescaleros, a tribe that had been at peace for several years, and that they had been enticed off the reservation by a man named Sanchez further strengthened Murphy's theory that there was more to the attack on the Price homestead than he had at first believed.

And though he had no proof, he was more convinced than ever that the murder of Travis at Doc Woods's had to, in some way, be tied to the Apaches' attack.

But why? Murphy started to contemplate the question, then stopped himself. He'd already spent far too many hours studying dozens of farfetched possibilities and all it had done was make his head hurt. He didn't have a clue who murdered Travis or why, but he did know who killed his wife and children seven days ago and he intended to go after them.

The renegade at the canyon who had earlier agreed to trade a horse for Kaetennae was probably Sanchez, but it was also possible that he was already dead, shot down by Murphy in the dark. The first thing in the morning, Murphy decided, he'd ride out and check the canyon.

Apaches usually carried their dead off for burying, but this bunch, afraid of pursuit, might not have, and though the bodies would be badly decomposed, the silver medallion the major mentioned would tell him if Sanchez was among them.

Perhaps Kaetennae was right and his brother Pionsenay would show up, but Murphy wasn't about to sit around

61

forever on that chance. He'd already spent too much time waiting for troops that didn't come. He had to do something—anything.

The front door to the jail burst open and the bald, pudgy bartender from the saloon down the street appeared. "Come quick, Sheriff. There's a fight, and they're bustin' up everything."

Murphy grabbed his hat and quickly passed the fat man in the street, running toward the saloon. Usually the occasional drunken brawls didn't amount to much, but if he could get there quickly enough, it might avoid any gunplay.

He reached the boardwalk, and a man flew out of the bat-wing saloon door, landing in the street. Murphy pulled out the Smith, stepped inside, and fired one round through the roof, which stopped the fight instantly and drew everyone's attention.

The place was a wreck. Most of the tables and chairs were overturned; there were bits of broken glass everywhere. The puffing bartender came through the door beside Murphy.

"Who started it?" Murphy asked in a low tone.

"Those two over there. The tall one with the mustache, he—"

A shot rang out, coming from up the street, followed by another much louder one. Murphy turned and stepped out of the saloon. He remembered the prisoner he'd left unguarded, and he ran toward the jail. He wasn't far from it when a yell stopped him.

"Hold her up or I'll blast you down."

The voice was Skeet's and Murphy searched the shadows for him. "It's me, Skeet. Al."

Skeet appeared in the street beyond the jail, holding his ten-gauge Greener. "Good thing you sung out or I'da blasted you for sure."

Murphy moved quickly into the jail. the Smith held

ready in his right hand. Kaetennae wasn't in his usual position in the corner of the cell, and it took Murphy a moment to locate him. The Indian lay prone under the narrow, wood-framed bed he never used.

"Are you hit?" Murphy asked.

Kaetennae's brown, almost black eyes were wide. He shook his head.

Skeet came in and Murphy turned to him, holstering his gun. "What happened? I was at the saloon and—"

"At the saloon?" Skeet angrily broke open his shotgun to replace the spent shell. "Fine sheriff you are, off drinkin' when you ought to a been here takin' care of things. Is that Indian shot? Where is he? I cain't see him nowhere."

"He's all right." Murphy glanced back at the cell. Kaetennae was pulling himself out from under the bunk. "There's no time. I've got to get back to the saloon. What—"

Christine and Moses stepped through the door. Murphy went on. "Tell me, Skeet. Tell me what happened!"

"Well, no use for you to be gettin' mad at me. I wasn't the—"

Christine interrupted. "I fixed supper for you and asked Skeet to bring it over."

"That's right," Skeet said. "An' I was comin' when I seen somebody out there by the door. At first I thought it was you, but then he see'd me comin' and he shot in the jail through the open door and went to runnin'. I got one barrel off at him, but he was too far. My scattergun ain't too good when it's too far."

Murphy's thoughts spun. No one was in the jail except Kaetennae, which meant the shot had to have been intended for him. The would-be assassin would have doubtless killed the renegade if Skeet hadn't shown up at just the wrong time.

The fight at the saloon must have been started to draw

Murphy away from the jail. The timing of the shooting and the brawl was too perfect to be a coincidence.

Murphy started for the door. He had to reach the saloon before the two men who had started the fight left. If they were in on the setup, and it looked like they had to be, they must know who Skeet had shot at. It might be the same man who'd killed Travis Price.

"Stay here, Moses," Murphy shouted over his shoulder. "Get a lantern, Skeet, and look for blood. You might have hit him with a pellet or two."

Murphy noticed that there were no horses tied to the hitching rail in front of the saloon as there had been earlier. He pulled his revolver out and looked over the batwing doors before entering. The two men were gone. Except for the piano player and the bartender, who were busily standing up tables and sweeping around them, everyone was gone.

He holstered the Smith and walked in. Both men looked up at him.

"Do you know the names of the men who started the fight? Do you know where they went?"

The barkeep wiped at some blood in the corner of his mouth. "Never saw 'em before. They left in a real big hurry right after you did. So did everybody else. Now who's gonna pay for all this?" He swung the broom around. "One of 'em slugged me and they went on. What was the shootin' about anyway?"

Murphy ignored the question. "You're sure you don't know them?"

The piano player set the neck of a broken bottle on a table. "Neither one of them was ever here before or we'd remember. They were strangers, probably just passing through."

"How'd the fight start?"

"Amongst each other first," the bartender said. "Then they started hittin' anybody and everybody."

"Did you see them ride off? Notice their horses? Was there anyone here who seemed to know them?"

Both men shook their heads. Murphy turned to go. "If you think of anything, anything at all, let me know."

Back at the jail, Murphy found Christine, Moses, and Skeet waiting for him. "Did you find any blood, Skeet?"

"Naw. I knew it was too far when I let her go. You still ain't told me what you was doin' down at the saloon, drinkin' when you ought to a been here tendin' to business. We'd just all like to know—"

"There was a fight," Murphy interrupted sharply, his patience wearing thin. "It was a planned fight to get me away from here. How well did you see the man you shot at?"

"Not much good. Like I done told you, I thought he was you."

"Was he wearing a hat? A high-crowned hat like some of the cowboys wear?"

"He had a hat for sure, but I don't know nothin' 'bout the crown. It's plumb dark out there and it was too far."

Murphy moved to Kaetennae's cell. The Indian had resumed his position in the corner and was watching him.

"Someone is going to a lot of trouble to try and kill you," Murphy said. "Why do you keep protecting them? Tell me what you know."

Kaetennae's gaze was steady. He offered no response, and Murphy finally turned and wearily sat down in his chair. He pushed his hat back and massaged his forehead with his fingers.

Christine stepped up to the desk. "What you need is a cup of coffee and something to eat. Come on over to the store. Moses and Skeet"—she glanced at them hopefully—"will stay here until you get back. I doubt anything else is going to happen tonight."

Murphy stood, pulling his hat back down to its usual position. "Sounds good. I guess there's not much else we can do for now."

He stopped by Skeet on his way out, putting his hand on the old man's bony shoulder. "Thanks. You're right. If it hadn't been for you I'd have lost a prisoner."

Murphy hesitated, wondering in view of the latest events whether his earlier decision to leave in the morning was the right thing to do. Yet what was the alternative? To sit around the jail, waiting for who knows how long until something else happened or someone else died?

"Moses and I are leaving at daybreak to hunt for Pionsenay Sanchez. Will you stay here and look after the place? Whoever we're dealing with may be back."

"Course I will," Skeet said. "Cain't do no worse 'n you. If'n they come again, they'll get a load of buckshot for their trouble. I'll be needin' my badge though. Ain't no such thing as a deputy what ain't got no badge. Remember when me and you and Moses took on half the county? Why I . . ."

Murphy waited patiently until Skeet finally finished. "Your old badge is in the top drawer." He looked at Moses, who stood by the door. "You'll be ready?"

"I be ready now. Right now."

CHAPTER 13

THE DUN COLT moved out smoothly beside Moses' huge, buckskin gelding. Murphy held the hackamore reins loosely in his left hand. He wanted the young horse to be sweet-mouthed, and it would be a month or more before he would replace the hackamore with a bit and bridle.

Moses put his buckskin into a trot, and Murphy allowed the big colt to follow along of his own accord. The horse had an easy gait and Murphy liked the way he moved. He might never be the horse the *grulla* was, but he'd more than do.

Fifteen minutes later the sun came up and Turrett lay far behind them. Murphy watched Moses, who was a little ahead, remembering the first time he'd met the man.

Skeet was driving McCormick freight wagons, which at that time was a dangerous job, due to the ongoing feud with another mercantile. Christine hired Murphy to go along with him, riding shotgun. Arriving at the fort one evening, they unhitched the mules and took them to the livery for the night. It was Moses who greeted them. He was post blacksmith and the biggest man Murphy had ever seen.

They shook hands, and Murphy still remembered how tiny his hand felt in Moses' gentle, yet firm grip and how much he had instantly liked, even admired, the man, all based on instincts that he didn't understand but had learned to trust.

Later, at Skeet's urging, Moses quit his job at the post and went to work as a driver for Christine at much better pay. He had relatives living in poverty in Alabama and hoped to save enough money to buy a piece of watered land so they could move out here and farm it. Fort Crosston and the Mescalero Indian Reservation would provide a ready market for their crops.

In the last year, Murphy had found his initial feelings about Moses Coffin to be correct. No one could ask for a better, more-loyal friend.

The day was warm and the miles long. Because Moses and Murphy knew where they were going, they didn't attempt to follow the Apaches' trail from the Price ranch, but headed in a straight northeasterly line toward the canyon and the *malpais*.

At noon, and not far from their destination, they dismounted and stretched their legs while their mounts grazed. Murphy was glad for the break. The few hours of constant riding had caused his arrow wound to ache and he needed to relax his shoulders.

He opened the saddlebags he'd borrowed from Skeet and took out a hard biscuit.

"You hungry?"

Moses took a drink from his canteen. "I got some food in my pack. You go ahead." He replaced the cork. "You think them Apaches you killed'll still be there?"

"Hard to say. If they are, between the heat, varmints, buzzards, and maggots, there may not be much left, but we can see if one of them has a silver medallion around his neck."

"Unless we find it, you still won't be knowin' if this Sanchez feller's there. One of them others could have took it."

"I thought of that, but I don't think they would have. Apaches believe a man enters the 'other world' in the same condition he left this one. When it's one of their own, they gather everything that belonged to him so he can take it with him."

Moses put his canteen strap over his saddle horn. "It

ain't rained none. We can pick up their trail. It's done been too long for us to catch 'em, but maybe we can see where they was headin'."

"Yeah. If nothing else, we can do that."

The two mounted and soon reached the entrance to the canyon where Murphy had come very close to losing his life. The day was much like that day: hot, clear, and still.

Murphy took the lead. He knew the Apaches' camp had been in the bottom of the canyon, but he wasn't sure how far down it was. The landscape looked different in the day than it had in the night.

A mile and a half farther the canyon bed widened and they rounded a bend. Thirty or more buzzards took to the air in one dark, turbulent mass. Their loud, flapping wings spooked the dun and he whirled into a long, high jump that almost threw Murphy from the saddle.

Moses' buckskin, frightened by the sudden move of the colt, turned with speed and agility uncommon for a horse his size and broke into a wild run. It was a few minutes before both riders were able to settle their mounts enough to return to the site. Moses turned to Murphy, grinning. "That hoss 'bout throw'd you."

Murphy rubbed his shoulder. The excitement hadn't helped his wound any. He smiled. "You didn't look like you were sitting none too good." Murphy pointed ahead. Three bodies lay around a dark spot that had been the Apaches' fire. "Looks like they're still here."

As they drew closer, the dun snorted and shied. Murphy dismounted, tied the horse to a root sticking out of the wash bank, and slowly walked toward the bodies, trying to prepare himself for the gruesome scene awaiting him. Moses stayed on the buckskin. It didn't take two people to look for the medallion.

The buzzards circled high above, gliding effortlessly through the air and waiting for the chance to resume their meal of human flesh. Murphy's inspection of the dead didn't take long.

He called to Moses. "The medallion's not on them. If I remember right, I hit another one. We better look around some."

Moses dismounted and helped search the area. Nearly an hour later they untied their horses, having found no sign of the wounded man or anything else.

Murphy mounted and looked at the sun, guessing there to be at least four hours of daylight left. He hadn't learned much, but at least he wouldn't waste his time chasing dead men. Odds were that Pionsenay Sanchez was very much alive.

Moses nudged the buckskin beside Murphy. "We gonna trail 'em? I remember where I last seen 'em ridin' over the top of the ridge."

Murphy took his hat off and wiped the sweat from the band. "I guess we better. Seems like the only thing left to do." He put his hat back on. "Don't you think it's strange we haven't heard about any other attacks? Seems like the Prices were the only ones the renegades were after. The major said Sanchez promised the Indians lots of plunder and whiskey."

"Don't make no sense. Surely don't. Maybe you shootin' some of 'em broke 'em up. Maybe the rest of 'em just went on back to the reservation. Ain't no way of knowin'. Them Apaches' tracks might tell us somethin'."

"I hope so," Murphy answered. "I really do hope so."

CHAPTER 14

TWO DAYS LATER, Murphy and Moses walked their tired mounts through the large, timbered gates of Fort Crosston.

They had followed the Apaches' trail until it disappeared into the ruts of the wagon road running between Turrett and the fort. There could be no doubt. The renegades had gone back to the reservation.

The two rode past the lamp-lit commissary and canteen on their way to the livery. Skeet had been right. The place did look deserted compared to the other times Murphy had been there. Moses stopped the buckskin and stepped down.

"I can tend to our horses if you be wantin' to find the major. It's gettin' late, must be ten o'clock or more."

Murphy slowly dismounted. He was stiff, and the long, hard trip had caused the steady ache in his shoulder to become almost unbearable. He patted the dun's neck. The young horse had done a good job, more than should have been expected of him, but his muscles weren't hardened for so much work so soon. He was completely worn out.

"No. I'll help feed and rub them down, then we'll both go and see the major."

The horses taken care of, they walked toward a lone white house located south of the entry gate. The house was the only wooden structure inside the fort—the others were all adobe—and it was the only building that had been painted.

Murphy knocked loudly on the ornately carved front door in the light of a bright lamp above him. He and Moses could have waited until morning to make the visit, avoiding the risk of waking the major up, but they'd ridden too long with too many unanswered questions wearing on their minds to wait any longer than they had to.

The Apaches had returned to the reservation, they were sure of it, and the major might now know a lot more than he did when he sent the letter with Skeet.

Major Hilleary, a tall, thin man dressed in uniform striped pants, a long-sleeved gray undershirt, and black suspenders, opened the door.

"Murphy. Al Murphy." He stepped out on the veranda and shook hands. "And Moses. It's so good to see you. Come in. Please come in. A drink is in order. From the looks of you the march has been a long one."

They removed their hats and followed the major in. "Hope we didn't wake you," Murphy said. "We just got in."

"Of course not. It would not matter if you had." He motioned toward a finely furnished parlor. "Sit down. Make yourselves comfortable. Which is it, scotch, bourbon, brandy, or wine?"

"Bourbon for me," Murphy said, still standing. Neither he nor Moses could bring himself to sit on the matching red velvet chairs in their dusty riding clothes.

"Moses?"

"Bourbon be just fine, thank you."

The major turned from a bottle-laden table and handed each of them a tall glass. "Sit down. Please, I insist. A little dust won't hurt the furniture."

Murphy and Moses reluctantly sat down. Murphy drank half his drink in one swallow, hoping the whiskey would relax him and dull the pain in his shoulder. The major poured himself a drink and sat across from them.

"I am happy you are here. Did Mr. Ames deliver my letter to you?"

Murphy nodded. "We got it." He told the major everything that had recently happened in Turrett County and how the Apaches' tracks had brought them here.

Major Hilleary took a sip of brandy and set the glass down. "You are right. The remaining renegades have indeed returned to the reservation and are in custody. One of them is wounded, a bullet through the elbow.

"They returned the night of Mr. Ames's departure for Turrett, but three days passed before their presence was discovered by my men. I immediately sent a messenger to Turrett with the updated report addressed to you, but you must have left before he arrived."

"Did you get Sanchez?" Murphy asked.

The major shook his head slowly. "No, I wish we had. The Sanchez family has a small, run-down farm located along the Little Bonito Creek, which flows adjacent to the western reservation boundary. Dominic Sanchez, who has been dead for many years, homesteaded the property. He was married to a Mescalero woman and that union produced six sons, the oldest of whom is Pionsenay.

"All of the boys except the youngest have been incarcerated here in the stockade at one time or another for various acts of misconduct, none of which were serious enough in nature to hold them for any length of time.

"The family has been a continual nuisance around the fort for years and, I suspect, a major contributor to the severe alcohol problem we have with the Indians, though I have been unable to attain any proof of that accusation."

The major uncrossed his legs and reached for his drink. "Immediately after learning about the return of the hostiles, I composed a squadron out of what few men I have left and surrounded the Sanchez farm. We were too late. Mrs. Sanchez, the elderly Apache mother of the six brothers, was the only one there.

"She admitted Pionsenay had been there, but said he had left the day before, taking his brothers with him. I questioned her thoroughly, trying to ascertain their probable destination, but with no results. I am convinced that she really doesn't know."

Murphy stood, drinking the last of the bourbon. "I know. They're going after Kaetennae."

The major nodded. "From what you have told me, that seems most probable."

Moses rose, looking at Murphy. "We best be goin'. Skeet's gonna need help. Hope we ain't too late."

Murphy set his glass on the table. "Major, did any of the Apaches you're holding say anything? Did they give any clue as to why they attacked the Prices and no one else?"

"I questioned each of them thoroughly. They said they were all drunk when they left the reservation with Sanchez."

He cleared his throat. "Apache society is based on war, raiding, and the accumulation of booty. Young Apache men confined to a reservation do not have the freedom to prove their manhood, their warrior capabilities, and their worth to the tribe.

"From what the renegades told me, Pionsenay was shrewd enough to use that cultural aspect to get them to go with him. The Price family was attacked under his direction. He told them there were large quantities of liquor in the barn and in the house."

The major stepped closer to Murphy. "Apparently it was Pionsenay Sanchez who killed Mrs. Price and the children. The Mescaleros said Travis was outside, bridling his horse, when they struck. Wounded, he mounted and rode a short distance, then stopped and began shouting obscenities in an effort to lure them away from his home.

"Sanchez and most of the renegades ran back to where they had tied their horses and gave chase. When they were unable to catch Travis before he reached the outskirts of Turrett, they returned to the ranch. The Apaches were angry about not being able to find the liquor they were promised, but it was Sanchez who in a rage brutally slaughtered the woman and children.

"After your battle with the renegades, which almost halved their number, the braves refused to follow Sanchez any longer and started back to the reservation. Apparently Sanchez, having lost his small war party, had little choice but to return with them."

Murphy thought back to the tracks he'd found at the homestead. They matched the story the Mescaleros had given the major and he believed the account was true. "Have the Sanchez brothers done any other killing?"

"Not that I am aware of. Several fights, a few with knives and one involving a pistol, I believe, but no one has been seriously hurt."

Murphy glanced at Moses, knowing that the big man's buckskin was one of the few horses around large enough to carry him. "Your horse able to start for Turrett tonight?"

"He be tired but he can do it if I help him some."

"Can I borrow a horse from you, Major? Mine's too far gone."

"Of course. I only wish I could do more. As I mentioned in my letter, my command is committed and I must retain the few soldiers I have left for the security of the post."

"I understand." Murphy looked at the liquor bottles on the table. The drink hadn't done much to ease his discomfort and he wondered if *he* was able to start back to Turrett tonight.

"Major, my shoulder's been bothering me some. Could I take a bottle with me? We've a hard ride ahead of us."

"Take it, Sheriff. Both of you take whatever you need. I'll have two field packs of rations prepared for you immediately."

"Thanks, Major," Murphy said. "I just hope we can get to Turrett soon enough."

CHAPTER 15

EIGHT MILES OF long, gentle slope up the eastern side of the mountain face was all that remained of Moses' and Murphy's eighty-mile trip to Turrett.

Fifteen hours had passed since leaving Fort Crosston, and in that time they had stopped only once to eat and water the horses. It had been thirty-six hours since either of them had slept. Murphy drank the last of the bourbon the major had given him forty miles back.

Moses, who had walked and jogged a good part of the journey to conserve his horse's strength, stopped and mounted. He wiped the stinging sweat out of his eyes with his handkerchief and looked up at the midafternoon sun.

"Won't be much longer now." He looked at Murphy, who was several feet in front of him, noticing a large, dark blotch on the back of his shirt. "Your wound done broke open. You be bleedin'."

Murphy didn't respond, but put the sorrel mare he'd borrowed at the fort into a trot. The bleeding, the racking pain in his shoulder that shot through him with each step the mare took, wasn't important. He had to reach Turrett. Perhaps Sanchez and his brothers hadn't made their move to rescue Kaetennae yet. Maybe there was still time to get ready for them.

Turrett came into view, and both horses picked up speed. A settlement meant rest, hay, and grain.

The town lay quiet. A buggy was parked in front of Doc Woods's home, a wagon stood by the loading ramp of the McCormick Mercantile, and a couple of horses were hitched in front of the saloon across from it. The scene was typical of most hot, lazy afternoons in Turrett.

Murphy and Moses stopped their horses by the hitching rail in front of the jail and stepped wearily to the ground. Skeet came out of the open doorway, holding the Greener. Murphy looked at him, waiting for the fusillade of words that should have already started but strangely had not. Something was wrong, very wrong.

"What is it, Skeet? What's happened?"

"The boy. They done got him. While you was off chasing 'em to who knows where, they took the boy and they're holdin' him."

"What boy? What are you talkin' about?"

"Sanchez." Skeet gestured behind him. "That Indian's brother, that's who! He's got Billy, you know, Sarah's little boy."

The news, on top of everything else that had happened in the last couple of weeks, was almost more than Murphy's frazzled nerves and tired mind could take. He stared at Skeet through wide, bloodshot eyes, unable to speak. Moses stepped beside Skeet and pointed toward the mercantile.

"Here come Miss Christine and Miss Sarah now."

Murphy looked to the side and over the top of his saddle at the two approaching women. He wrapped the sorrel's reins once around the hitching rail and stepped around it, the full impact of what Skeet had said finally hitting him. He saw the ghastly scene of the two small Price children heaped in a corner of the room and covered with blood. The man who was responsible for those brutal murders had Billy and he wouldn't hesitate to bash his head in, too, if he hadn't already.

Christine helped Sarah up on the narrow boardwalk. The woman's face was flushed and she was obviously beside herself with grief. Murphy remembered seeing her for the first time shortly after her husband's death and she'd had that same desperate, broken expression on her face then. He took her other arm and helped Christine seat her inside the jail.

Murphy kneeled in front of Sarah and took her hand in his. He knew that if Sanchez had taken Billy like Skeet said, the chances of getting the boy back alive were slim to none, but he wasn't about to tell her that. What she needed, what they all needed, was hope.

"Skeet told me about Billy. He'll be all right. We'll get him back, I promise you that."

Sarah took a crumpled note out of her hand and gave it to him. Murphy read it out loud.

"will trad boy for our bruther at skelton crosing in 2 days. do not follo or i will kill boy."

Murphy raised up, looking at Christine. "What happened? Where did you find this?"

"Yesterday afternoon Billy went riding down by the creek at the ranch. You know how he loves to play there. When he didn't come home by suppertime, Sarah and one of the ranch hands went to look for him. They found the note pinned to a tree."

"No one tried to follow them, did they?"

Christine shook her head. "They were afraid to."

Murphy moved to Kaetennae's cell. The Indian stared at him from the corner. "I wish I had killed you. I should have let Moses kill you. If anything—" He caught himself, realizing Sarah was listening. He turned and looked at her. Her head was down, her face in her hands.

"What we gonna do?" Moses asked.

Murphy went to his desk and sat down. He was tired, so very tired. He wanted it all to end. Wanted to walk out in the street and face them all with the Smith pounding against the back of his hand as he pulled the trigger. Fight Sanchez and his brothers. Fight whoever had murdered Travis Price.

But there would be no fight to end it, not yet. Murphy raised his head. "Nothing else we can do. We'll trade."

"Gonna have to leave first light in the mornin'," Skeet said. "Skeleton Crossin's more'n twenty miles from here. That's where they was that big fight with them Apaches a long time ago, you know. More'n a hundred was killed there. Crosston, that's who Fort Crosston's named after, he and more'n half his bunch was wiped out. They's still some bones layin' around them hills."

Murphy looked at Christine. "When is your next freight run to the fort?"

"Not for a while. Not long after you left, a messenger arrived with a letter from Major Hilleary. He said that with his command gone, he had enough supplies to last a month or more. He also said the Apaches who attacked the Price place had returned to the reservation and he has them under arrest."

"I know," Murphy said. "Moses and I just came from there."

Murphy explained everything he and Moses had learned at the fort, and why he was riding the sorrel mare instead of the dun. He finished and looked out the open door for several minutes. A gust of wind hit and the door creaked loudly, swinging back and forth on rusty hinges. No one spoke.

The beginning of an idea was forming in Murphy's head and he was trying to make his dull, weary mind put the pieces together. Sanchez might make a fair trade for Kaetennae if Billy was still alive, but Murphy doubted it. And even if the man did turn the child over, he shouldn't be allowed to get away a second time. Murphy needed an edge, something to swing the odds of how things went at Skeleton Crossing in his favor.

At last he turned. "Skeet, can you get a team and wagon to Skeleton Crossing?"

"Ought to be able to. The old road to the fort went

through there a long time ago and they's a few ranches out that way still usin' it some. What we need with a wagon? A wagon ain't gonna do us no good. Just make the goin' slow, that's all it'd do."

Murphy ignored him and glanced at Christine. "I need three of your horses, two of them the fastest you have. One of them is for Moses, so make him as big as you can, and—and another one that can barely walk. Maybe something real old. We'll need to load the wagon tonight."

"Load it with what?" Skeet asked. "Ain't no use in us takin' a bunch of stuff with us. It'll just make the goin' slower. This ain't no campin' trip, you know. We're suppose to be goin' after Billy."

"I need it loaded with boxes," Murphy continued, "empty boxes, especially liquor boxes." He pointed at Moses. "Go to the saloon and get all of them you can—empty barrels too. Take the bottles out of new cases if you have to. Tell the barkeep I have to have them.

"Christine, do you have any rifle shipping crates?"

"Yes. There's a few. I keep them to store things in."

"Get them. I want the wagon to look like it's loaded level-full of whiskey, rifles, and foodstuffs."

Moses moved from the stove to the center of the room. Thick trail dust covered his black face and hands, making him look something like a giant ghost. "I seen it done once before in the army." A thin smile spread on his lips. "You gonna bait 'em. Make 'em want somethin' so bad they's got to have it so it'll take they eyes off of what we be doin' and we can ambush 'em."

Murphy nodded. "Something like that." He glanced at Sarah. Her eyes met his and he noticed a change in them, a glimmer of hope that hadn't been there before.

"If it doesn't work," he said, "we've lost nothing. We'll still make the trade. We'll get Billy back."

Murphy stepped to his desk and took out a piece of paper. "How well do you know the country around the crossing, Skeet?"

"I know'd it all right. Use to have to go through there years back. Some of it's pretty dang rough."

"Help me put a map together, high places, flats, hills, adjacent canyons, arroyos—anything and everything you can remember about it."

Christine took Sarah by the hand and they rose from their chairs. "We'll get busy. I'll send the clerk out for the horses and start getting the boxes ready. We'll have dinner ready for everyone at dark."

She eyed Murphy. "I'm sending Doc Woods over to look at your back. You've been bleeding."

"Just a little."

"A little is too much. Tonight, you and Moses need to take a bath and get all the rest you can. If you don't, from the looks of you, you won't be able to do much of anything tomorrow."

"We'll be ready, won't we, Moses?"

Moses started out the door. "Got to be. We done got to be ready."

CHAPTER 16

AL MURPHY SAT in his chair, watching the smoke from his cigarette spiral lazily upward in the light of the lamp above him. His Smith, which he'd just finished cleaning, and a fairly new Colt in the same caliber lay on the desk in front of him, loaded and ready.

He felt good, considering the shape he had been in yesterday, and he marveled at what a hot bath, a few hours' sleep, and a fresh set of clothes could do for a man. Doc Woods had restitched and bandaged his arrow wound, and though his shoulder was sore, the constant pain was gone.

The sound of an approaching wagon and team reached Murphy and he rose, flicking the butt of his cigarette on the floor and stamping it out. He holstered the Smith, put the Colt in his waistband, and reached for the cell keys hanging on the rock wall behind him.

"All right," he said, opening Kaetennae's cell door. "It's time to go and meet the brother you're so fond of. You give me any trouble and you'll be gumming mush for the rest of your life. There won't be a tooth left in your head."

Skeet and Moses walked through the door, followed by Christine and Sarah. Murphy finished handcuffing Kaetennae's hands behind his back and left him lying facedown on the floor.

"Everythin's ready," Skeet said. "It's an hour or better till sunup, but we might just as well get goin'. Don't want to be late, you know."

"Your shotgun ready, Skeet?" Murphy asked.

"Ah, course it is. Don't you think I got enough sense to load my own gun? Why, I was loadin' guns 'fore you was born. Don't be askin' me about my gun, you tend to your own gun. I . . ."

Murphy moved to the gun rack in the corner of the room and took down the only two rifles on it: the .44 Henry he'd taken from Kaetennae and an old .56 caliber repeating Spencer. He handed the latter to Moses, along with a box of shells. "You might need this."

"I got my Sharps. It be good for most anythin'."

"I know, but it's a single shot and it wouldn't hurt to carry them both. Depending on how things turn out, it'll be up to you to get to Billy. You know what to do?"

"Surely do. I wait here till a while after you leave, then follow along, stayin' out of sight but where I can keep an eye on you with my spyglass.

"At the crossin' I start lookin' for 'em while they's lookin' at you. If most of 'em goes for the wagon, I go for Billy. If'n they don't, I just ride around so they don't see me and meet up with you a few miles on past the crossin'."

Murphy nodded. He turned to Kaetennae's cell. The man lay sprawled as he'd left him. "I guess we're as ready as we can get. Let's load him up."

Outside, Murphy and Moses worked to sandwich and hide Kaetennae between the boxes in the bed of the wagon. The task finished, Murphy climbed out to get the Henry and a box of ammunition. Christine met him at the front door of the jail with both.

"I wish you had deputized a few of the ranch hands to go with you. They all care about Billy, and a few of them are good shots."

"I know. I'd like to take a posse with me. If I'd done that the first time I went after Sanchez from the Price place, he wouldn't be holding Billy now. He'd be dead or in jail.

"But there's barely enough room left in the wagon now for Kaetennae and me. More men on horses might spook Sanchez and we'd lose Billy. No, Skeet and me and Moses are enough. We were enough once before, remember?"

Christine started to smile, then stopped. She knew he was referring to the Turrett County war, the final gun battle. "I remember. You were shot to pieces and it's a wonder you lived through it."

Sarah edged past Christine. Her voice was strong, steady. "Whatever happens, Al, I know that you, Skeet, and Moses will do your best to bring Billy back."

Murphy touched her cheek. "Keep hoping, believing."

"We gonna sit around here all day jawin'?" Skeet shouted from the wagon seat. "It's purt near time for the mules to be watered and fed again. They're gettin' old just standin' here. If you don't get in this wagon, I'm leavin' without you. Prob'ly don't need ya nohow. All you want to do is . . ."

Murphy held Christine's hand briefly and climbed in the back of the wagon just as Skeet popped the reins and the four mules leaned into their harness. The suddenness of the jolt almost threw Murphy out, would have, if he hadn't grabbed one of the ropes holding the boxes in place. He watched Christine and Sarah until the darkness took them from his sight, then settled in beside Kaetennae.

The numerous empty boxes creaked loudly with the motion of the wagon, and Murphy wondered if they should have placed rocks in them to hold them down better. He looked at the three horses tied behind the wagon, only able to see their heads clearly.

Two of them were some of Christine's best, horses that anyone would be proud to own. The third was an old, swaybacked, smooth-mouthed roan that could barely walk. If the ambush didn't work, if Pionsenay Sanchez didn't take the bait and attack the wagon, they'd put Kaetennae on the roan and try to make the trade. Once Billy was safe, Murphy and Skeet could saddle and mount the two fast horses and, along with Moses, chase Sanchez and his brothers down.

Kaetennae sat quietly, unmoving. Murphy gazed up at the stars, thoughtfully going over his plan. If Sanchez could be trusted to make a fair trade, the wagon and ambush preparations were unnecessary.

But Murphy knew he wasn't the only one who could think up tricks and traps. There was no telling what Sanchez had in mind for the day, no way of knowing if Billy was even alive, and the wagon loaded with the appearance of irresistible plunder might serve to throw the man off, cause him to do things he hadn't intended.

As far as Murphy knew, five men held Billy. Pionsenay and his four brothers. If they decided to attack the wagon, it was unlikely that more than one of them would stay behind with the small boy. Moses' job was to handle that man and rescue Billy.

Murphy had done what he could to see that Moses knew where to look. He and Skeet had gone over every detail of their crude map with him, pointing out draws, hills, gullies, and a nearby alkaline spring that seemed to be the most probable place for Sanchez and his brothers to be at.

With luck, while the kidnappers' attention was focused on the wagon and horses, Moses would spot them. When and if they made their move, he'd make his.

The night began to fade into day. Murphy scanned the piñon-scattered, grassy slope behind for a glimpse of Moses, but could not locate him. He glanced to his side at Kaetennae. The Indian's cruel, beady eyes and twisted expression were more defiant than ever. He was sure to cause trouble if given the opportunity.

Murphy's thoughts turned to Billy. He remembered the last time he'd seen him while lying in bed at Christine's. The boy was smiling, ready to chase after the outlaws.

It wasn't right that he should have to go through this. Pionsenay Sanchez wasn't a man. He was a dog, a rabid dog that needed killing, and if at all possible, Murphy intended to do just that.

Four hours later they were within three miles of Skeleton Crossing. The day was hot and clear. Murphy had seen

Moses only once, and that for an instant when the sun's glare reflected off his telescope. The big man was either very good at concealing his movements or something had happened to him.

Murphy took his bandanna from his hip pocket, rolled it, and gagged Kaetennae tightly. He then reluctantly spread a tarp over them. The tarp would trap the hot air, creating an uncomfortable oven, but there was no help for it: Sanchez might be on a hill with a spyglass of his own.

Two barrels were positioned on either side of Murphy. The sides had been cut out so he could get in them and look out through several small drilled holes. He crawled into each of them, finding that he could see surprisingly well except directly in front and back.

Sweat started to bead his face and he sat back in the wagon bed, resting against a box and facing Kaetennae. There was nothing left to do but wait.

Sanchez had not mentioned in his note a time of day for the trade, and Murphy could only hope he was here, having spent the night somewhere nearby, possibly by the spring Skeet had pointed out on the map.

Skeet was supposed to hold the mules in a slow walk and drive the wagon straight through. He hadn't said anything, no one had, but should the ambush work, Skeet was the one who faced the greatest danger. Sitting up on the open wagon seat, he was an easy target.

The air under the tarp was hot and thick and rank with the odor of Kaetennae, who hadn't bathed in no telling when. Murphy wondered how long he was going to be able to stand it.

Several light taps hit the tarp, sounding like a sprinkle of large raindrops or hail. Skeet had pitched a handful of gravel over his shoulder, Murphy knew. It was the signal that Sanchez was coming.

Murphy moved to the right barrel and looked out the holes, seeing nothing. He turned swiftly to the left barrel and saw two mounted men hundreds of yards away approaching the wagon at an angle from the front. Something gleamed on the leading man's chest, and Murphy guessed it to be the medallion Pionsenay was known to wear.

Fear struck Murphy. Terrifying fear. The guts of the plan was that Pionsenay would leave only one of his brothers behind with Billy, two at the most. There was no way Moses was going to be able to handle three armed men and rescue the boy.

His great plan might cost Billy his life. If the two brothers tried to take the wagon, which it was certain they were coming to do, Murphy had no choice but to show his hand and fight. If Billy was alive, his life was hanging by a thread, a very thin thread, and Murphy was responsible for it.

Murphy wiped the pouring sweat out of his eyes with his shirtsleeve and looked through each hole in the barrel. He spotted two more men angling in from behind, men with long, black hair who were closer than the first two.

The tension in him eased somewhat. That left one man with Billy, and the four riders were coming in from the west, the same direction the wagon had come from. Moses wouldn't have to circle around to locate Billy. The boy had to be somewhere between him and the wagon.

"Whoa, you mules," Skeet hollered. The wagon slowed to a stop. Murphy crawled out of the barrel and squatted to a ready position on his feet, taking the Smith in his right hand and the Colt in his left. The thud of horse hooves came.

"Howdy," Skeet said. "It's sure enough a hot one today, ain't it? Where you fellows headed?"

Part of the plan was for Skeet to stall Sanchez as long as possible, giving Moses time to locate Billy. There was a pause and Murphy heard a horse walk around the wagon and stop.

"Where you go with guns, whiskey, and horses?"

At the sound of his brother's voice, Kaetennae squirmed and tried to yell through his gag. Murphy lashed out at him with amazing speed, hitting him on the side of his head just above the ear with the barrel of the Smith and rendering him unconscious. The click of the hammer on a gun being cocked was instant, coming from where the man had spoken.

"What you got in there?"

"Ah . . . well, that's my old hound Betsy. She's been kinda sick and I keep that there tarp over her to keep the sun off'n her. 'Bout my whiskey and guns—I got a lot more than this, you know, hid back in the hills. I'm a trader. If you're wantin' to—"

The report of a shot came from the west, making a thunderous roar. It was Moses' big .50-90 Sharps. Murphy jumped straight up. The tarp slid off his back while he fired the Smith and the Colt simultaneously at the two mounted men at the rear of the wagon, then he spun on his heels to face the front two without taking the time to see if his shots had hit or missed.

A gun went off behind him. To the right of Skeet a man fired a rifle, and Murphy pointed the Smith at him and pulled the trigger double-action. He cocked the Colt in his left hand and had started to swing it to the man on Skeet's left when Skeet's Greener thundered and the man was blown off the back of his horse.

Murphy looked to the right. The man he'd shot was down. He swung around to see what had happened to the two men in the rear; one of them, obviously wounded, was still mounted and about to shoot his revolver. Murphy threw a quick shot at him and saw the bullet hit him high in the chest. The man's pistol went off as he slid from the saddle.

For the first time Murphy noticed that the wagon was lurching back and forth as the startled mules tried to pull it against the brake. He leaped out and ran around the wagon, making sure all four men were dead.

The last one he checked wore a silver medallion around his neck. Skeet's load of buckshot had hit Pionsenay Sanchez full in the stomach, nearly cutting him in two.

The air was filled with the stench of gunpowder. Murphy looked up at Skeet. The little man was slumped to the side of the wagon seat, and blood covered the side of his shirt.

Murphy quickly climbed the wagon wheel. "Skeet!"

Skeet raised his head. "No use for you to holler at me. I ain't deaf, you know."

"Lay down on the seat so I can take a look."

Skeet gestured with his arm across the flat to the west. "Ain't that a sight a man'll never forget?"

Murphy looked to see Moses riding in a canter toward them with Billy sitting on the fork of his saddle.

Murphy smiled. He'd never been a religious man, yet he silently thanked the Lord he'd heard about as a child. He couldn't help the feeling that their good fortune was something more than plain luck.

Moses stopped by the mules and swung Billy to the ground. The boy took a few steps and on seeing Pionsenay Sanchez's body, stood stone still, his eyes frozen to the gruesome sight. Murphy stepped out of the wagon and kneeled beside the boy, turning him away. Billy's face was badly bruised and his lips cut, no doubt from beatings by Sanchez and his brothers.

"It's over, Billy," Murphy said. "Everything will be fine. Your mother is waiting for us in town. You'll be home with her tonight."

A tear slid down Billy's cheek. "I knew you'd come, Sheriff."

"I had to." Murphy hugged the boy. "You're my best deputy."

He stood and looked at Moses, who had dismounted. "Help me get Skeet down. He's been hit."

Skeet groaned as Moses lifted him from the wagon to the ground. "Be more careful. I ain't no sack a taters, you know."

Moses smiled and gently laid him down, glancing at Murphy. "Skeet ain't hurt too bad. He talks real good."

Murphy opened Skeet's shirt, finding that a bullet had made an ugly furrow an inch deep along his side. The wound didn't look too serious, if they could get the bleeding stopped.

He stepped to the wagon bed. Christine had twice reminded him last night that she'd packed some bandages in a food basket. He climbed in the back to look for it and pulled the tarp off Kaetennae. The man lay in a pool of blood. A stray round that must have been fired by one of his brothers had struck him in the forehead.

There was no remorse in Murphy. He quickly pitched the tarp back over the body. "Where's the basket Christine sent?"

"You never know nothin', do ya." Skeet grumbled. "It's under the wagon seat. A man'd bleed to death, waitin' on you. That's the trouble with young folks, they don't know nothin', cain't do nothin'. Why, I remember . . ."

CHAPTER 17

MURPHY PULLED THE young dun up on the ridge overlooking the valley where the Price homestead lay, and the horse lowered his head and scratched the nose band on the rope hackamore against his front leg. Major Hilleary had sent the horse along with a family traveling through Turrett on their way to Arizona Territory, and Murphy was glad to have him back.

The air was still and the morning sky clear. Four days had passed since the fight with the Sanchez brothers at Skeleton Crossing, and August had turned into the first week of September. Billy was home safe and Skeet was doing fine, spending most of his time at the jail or at the store with Moses.

Murphy should have felt relieved, even happy, but he wasn't. Instead he was restless over his inability to put the rest of the pieces of the puzzle together.

Sanchez and the Apaches hadn't been responsible for the murder of Travis Price in Doc Woods's home. According to Major Hilleary, they were on their way back to the reservation at the time. Someone else had to have killed him, probably the same man who tried to kill Kaetennae in the jail.

Who and why?

The questions consumed all of Murphy's waking moments. The attack on the Price family by Sanchez and the Mescaleros didn't make any more sense than the murder of Travis. Someone else had to be behind the attacks.

Murphy nudged the dun into a walk down the slope. He hoped a thorough search of the Price place might provide

91

a clue he'd overlooked earlier, though he wasn't too anxious to go back in the house and have the blood-spattered walls remind him of scenes he wished to forget.

He'd already visited most of the neighboring ranches, and if any of them had any animosity toward the Prices, it was well hidden.

The McCormick Mercantile records showed Price was in debt thirty-two dollars and seventy cents, not an unusual amount for a small rancher with a family. Most owed twice that, and Travis had always paid his bill in full when he sold his calves in the fall.

A check at the bank did turn up an interesting fact. Almost three months ago, Travis had requested a loan for fifteen hundred dollars. The banker had offered him three hundred against his property and another two on his cattle, but Travis refused it, saying he had to have the full fifteen to send to a relative who was ill.

Murphy was trying to find out who that relative was so he could notify him of Travis's death and possibly find out something that would add to Murphy's investigation. There was a chance that there might be a letter or something inside the Price home that would help him.

The dun snorted and shied away from the rectangle of fire-blackened debris which was all that was left of the Prices' two-room shack. Murphy dismounted, tied the horse to a rail in front of the barn, and slowly walked around it.

He kneeled and handled the charcoal, then stepped through it and raised a large piece of tin. There was no warmth beneath it. The fire, which had been a hot one, was several days old.

Murphy continued to walk around in the ashes, occasionally using the toe of his boot to uncover a metal cup or pan while trying to think of a reason why anyone would want to burn the place down.

Lightning could have started the fire, or a few curious

kids might have come by and set it ablaze just to watch it burn. But more likely, the fire was started by someone who wanted to make sure there was nothing inside that could implicate him.

Murphy searched the area. Cattle had milled around the place, obliterating any tracks that might have been left. He looked inside the barn. Varmints had eaten what was left of the milk cow the Apaches had butchered, and finding nothing else, Murphy mounted and arrived in Turrett a little before noon.

Skeet, moving stiff and slow from his wound, stepped out of the jail as Murpy dismounted and tied the reins.

"How come you never told nobody you had you a girl-friend. Christine was here a while ago and she don't look the none too happy. You ought to have told her 'stead of leadin' her on, the way you been doin'."

"If I was younger and my side didn't hurt so much, I'd learn you how to treat a woman better 'n that. Right out here in the street I'd learn you. I'd—"

"Skeet!" Murphy stepped up on the porch. "What are you talking about?"

"I'm talkin' 'bout your lady friend, that's what. The one what you ain't told nobody about."

"I haven't got a girl!" Murphy's voice lowered. "Except maybe Christine."

"No use in you lyin' to me. Me and Moses done seen her when she got off the stage in front of the store. First thing she done was go to askin' about you. She's right purty too, but you oughtn't do Christine that away. I'm a mind to get my scattergun and pepper a little sense into your backside. You ought to be . . ."

Murphy turned and headed for the store. Skeet's mind was made up, and it might take hours to change it and figure out what he was saying.

Moses stepped out of the store with two sacks of flour in

his arms, almost running into Murphy. The big man's look was cool.

"I don't have a girlfriend," Murphy muttered in defense, then walked into the store. A slender woman, perhaps in her early thirties, with brown, wavy hair, gray eyes, and a few freckles on her nose, was standing at the counter beside Christine. She watched him approach and held her hand out.

"Sheriff Murphy?"

"Yes." Murphy shook her hand briefly. "What can I do for you?"

"I thought you two knew each other," Christine interrupted, taking her hands off her hips.

"Oh, no," the woman said. "We've never met. I didn't mean to give you that impression. Sheriff, I'm Jenny Whickers."

Murphy glanced at Christine with an amused twinkle in his eyes. He turned to the woman. "How can I help you?"

"I don't mean to be rude, but could I talk to you in private?"

Christine went behind the counter and opened the door leading to her quarters in back. "You're welcome to use my kitchen."

Murphy nodded for Jenny to follow her. He winked at Christine before shutting the door and she blushed red. At the table, he pulled out a chair for the woman and stepped around to sit across from her. She took a letter from her purse.

"Sheriff, do you know Travis Price?"

"Yes, I knew him."

"Knew him?" Her eyes widened. "Has something happened to him?"

Murphy nodded. "Travis, his wife, and their two children are dead."

Tears formed in Jenny's eyes and her already pale complexion grew whiter. Her hands trembled and it was a moment before she could speak. "My maiden name is Price. I'm Travis's sister."

Questions started to form in Murphy's mind. He wondered if this woman could be the relative who was ill, the one Travis had tried to borrow the money at the bank for, yet he held his tongue, waiting for her to regain her composure and tell him more.

"How did they die?"

"Apaches, but I think there's a lot more to it than that. Travis made it into town after the attack. He might have lived, but someone murdered him while he was in bed at the Doc's."

She held up the letter. "I received this from Travis three months ago. My health is poor, and Travis was going to send me money to get treatment back east. He said to send this letter to you if I didn't receive the money from him by September the first. I was sure something was wrong— that's why I took the stage here from Mesa and brought the letter myself."

"Mesa, Arizona? Mormon country?"

She nodded.

"Where's your husband?"

"He was killed in a mine accident a year and a half ago. We have no children."

Murphy took the handwritten letter from her and opened it, reading silently.

My dearest sister Jenny,

I am sorry to hear you are ailing. It will take me a while to get hold of the money you are needing, but I am sure to be getting it soon. If you don't have it by the first of September, or have not heard from me, there is a spot by a lone cedar tree on top of a hill east of my ranch that will tell everything.

Send this letter to Sheriff Murphy at Turrett. He will know what to do. Do not tell no one else about it.

Your loving brother,
T/P

Murphy returned the letter to the envelope. "Can I keep this?"

"Yes." Jenny's eyes were red and puffy and she looked faint. Her voice was soft. "I haven't seen Travis in years. He'd written about his wife and two girls. I never met them. I hated to ask him for money, but there was no one else to turn to. Do you think his trying to raise the money somehow caused his death?"

"Of course not," Murphy lied. "I don't know why he was killed, but I'm sure it didn't have anything to do with the money."

Murphy stood. "I'm going to take a ride out and see if I can find that cedar tree your brother mentioned. I want you to stay here with Christine. You can trust her with everything you've told me. Travis was right, though. It'd be better if you didn't talk to anyone else about any of this."

Murphy opened the door and motioned for Christine to join them. He shut the door after her. "Christine, Miss Whickers is Travis Price's sister. I told her she could trust you. Her health isn't good and I asked her to stay here with you. I have to take a ride back out to the Price place. I should get back a little after dark.

Christine took a step closer beside Jenny. "We'll be fine. You go ahead."

Murphy started to leave, then turned. He grinned and slowly rubbed his chin. "Seems like Moses and Skeet have the wrong idea about some things. I'd appreciate it if you'd straighten them out before one of them shoots me and the other breaks me in two."

Christine turned to hide her embarrassment and moved toward the cookstove in the corner. "I'll take care of it."

CHAPTER 18

MURPHY SPURRED THE dun in an easy lope. The long hard ride he and Moses had taken to Fort Crosston a couple of weeks ago was more than the young horse should have been put through, yet those miles had taught him a great deal. He handled well and there was no buck in him. It wouldn't be another month or two, Murphy thought, before he was a seasoned, dependable riding horse.

A hill with a lone cedar tree on it. Murphy wondered how hard the hill would be to find. Travis must have thought it would stand out enough that no further description was necessary. What would he find there?

More and more, Murphy believed that the money Travis needed for his sister was a factor in his death. Travis knew his life was in danger, otherwise he wouldn't have told Jenny to send the letter to Turrett.

Murphy remembered the letter Major Hilleary had sent to Turrett with Skeet. Among other things, it said bootlegging to the Indians was on the rise. When he and Moses made it to Fort Crosston, the major said that Sanchez had told his followers there were large amounts of liquor in the Price house and in the barn.

Did Sanchez just make up the story to get the Mescaleros who were with him to attack, or was it possible that he really believed the liquor was there? Travis needed money and in his desperation might have done most anything to get it. Maybe Travis Price was running a still.

Murphy blinked and rubbed his eyes, not wanting to give much credence to speculations. He shifted his thoughts to the task before him and reached back to touch the short shovel he'd tied behind the cantle on his saddle.

A tree and hill wouldn't explain anything. Travis must have buried something there. After weeks of frustration and worry, there was a good chance that Travis's foresight was about to tell him what he so desperately needed to know.

The letter said the hill was east of the ranch. How far, one mile—ten?

Murphy stopped the dun in the same spot he'd been this morning, on the ridge overlooking the Price ranch. He scanned the valley east of the home place, immediately spotting the hill Travis had described.

It was the only hill in the valley, not much more than a swell really, and a lone, green tree stood on top of it. The distance was too far to tell if the tree was a cedar or juniper, but it had to be the right place. Murphy marveled at how many times he had looked at the hill without noticing or remembering it.

Thirty minutes later Murphy dismounted and thoroughly inspected the gnarled cedar, finding nothing unusual about it. He scanned the land around him to see if anyone was watching, then took his shovel off the saddle and began to probe the earth for a soft spot.

The grama grass was thick, and if Travis had buried something here, he had carefully fitted the sod back so his work didn't show. Presently, close to the base of the tree, the shovel almost disappeared under Murphy's boot, striking something hard.

More digging unearthed a coffee can. Inside the can was a tightly capped bottle, and inside the bottle was a piece of rolled paper with a string tied around it. Murphy pulled the string off the end, sat down on the grass, and unrolled the paper.

Sheriff,
    You reading this probly means I am dead, killed by Clyde

Harrelson or his foreman, Sandy Clayton. The gunfight at the Bar X between Ben Simson and Clyde was plain murder. I seen it. Ben was not carrying a gun. Clyde and Sandy both pulled down on him and shot him like you would a dog. Clyde has a whiskey still hid in a canyon, and Ben was one of his runners to the reservation.

I work for Clyde some and tried to borrow some money from him. He would not give me none. I told him I would tell you about the killing and the still if he did not give me the money. He said he would in a few weeks. I am afraid he will not do it and will shoot me. My wife does not know about none of this. Hope you and others will help her what you can.

T/P

Murphy let the letter fall in his lap. His thoughts were on the day in June he rode to the Bar X to investigate the shooting. When Murphy had stopped by the Prices' and told Travis where he'd been and what had happened, the man hadn't commented on any of it.

Murphy wondered whether Travis was already blackmailing Clyde that night or did it occur to Travis after Murphy's visit.

Travis was murdered by Clyde or Sandy because of what he threatened to tell about the bootlegging and the murder. But where did Sanchez and the Apaches fit in?

Murphy reflected on what he'd learned for some time before finally deciding that Sanchez had to have in some way been connected to Clyde Harrelson, probably in the bootlegging business. Clyde had probably hired the man to kill Travis and make it look like the Apaches had done it—or Sanchez could have taken it upon himself to recruit them.

It was Clyde who had wanted to lynch Kaetennae, and it must have been Clyde or Sandy who had staged the fight in the saloon and shot at Kaetennae in the jail, afraid that he would talk. The rancher was probably also responsible for the house fire. Maybe Travis had told Clyde he had hidden a note or something, thinking he was safeguarding himself. If only Travis had known how wrong he was.

The sun started to sink into the horizon. Murphy carefully folded the paper, pocketed it, and got to his feet. Travis's letter had given him all the pieces to the puzzle except one. The death of his wife and children. According to the note, Mrs. Travis didn't know anything about the Simson killing, the still, or the blackmail. But maybe Clyde Harrelson either did not know that or didn't believe it.

It was hard for Murphy to believe that Clyde was behind the whole family's deaths. Most ranchers were a tough, hard-nosed lot, and Harrelson was obviously into more than just ranching—but when it came to women and children, the line was drawn and few men would cross it.

Harrelson had arrived in Turrett not long after Murphy. The talk was that he'd sold a ranch in Colorado and moved here for the warm climate. He rarely came to town and Murphy had never had a conversation with him, discounting the night of the lynching party and the day he'd been to the ranch to investigate the shooting of Ben Simson.

Murphy had only met Sandy Clayton once, the day in June at the Bar X, and had instinctively disliked him. He was a tall, thin man with a drooping red mustache and small, restless blue eyes.

And he had the look of a gunfighter. Murphy had noticed the shortened, smoothly rounded hammer on Clayton's single-action Colt that allowed the gun to be slip-shot with the thumb when the trigger was tied back or removed. A practiced man could fire six shots into the space of a playing card fifteen feet away in less than three seconds or the gun could be fanned for even greater speed with less accuracy.

Murphy tied his shovel behind the saddle, mounted, and started the dun in the direction of the Bar X. A few minutes later he changed his mind and turned the horse back toward Turrett.

Someone else had to know what he now knew, and where he was going. If he was killed trying to arrest Clyde and Sandy and his body disposed of, the two men might never be brought to justice.

An hour and a half after dark Murphy unsaddled the dun, put him in the corral behind the jail, and fed him. Skeet and Moses weren't at the jail, and Murphy guessed they were either at Christine's or playing cards in the small bunkhouse behind the store.

He knocked on the outside door to Christine's quarters. She opened it and he stepped through. Jenny, who was seated at the kitchen table, stood. "Did you find the tree?"

Murphy hesitated a moment. He didn't want her to have to live with the fact that her request for money had, in a way, killed her brother.

"I found it. Travis buried a note there. The paper was wet and I was barely able to read it before it fell apart in my hands.

"Travis was murdered by a neighboring rancher who wanted his land. I think he hired a man to do it and make it look like it was a random raid by renegade Apaches. Travis knew he and his family were in danger and was shrewd enough to write to you and leave the note by the tree."

"Who was it?" Christine interrupted, handing Murphy a cup of coffee.

"Clyde Harrelson at the Bar X, or his foreman Sandy Clayton." He took a sip from the hot cup. Jenny sat down weakly, holding her face in her hands.

"Christine," Murphy said. "Will you come with me over to the jail? I need you to do a couple of things while I'm gone."

Christine took her shawl from the back of a chair and wrapped it over her shoulders. She looked at Jenny. "I'll be right back. You look very tired. If you'd like, go on into the bedroom and lie down. I want you to sleep there tonight."

"Thank you." Jenny stood. "I do feel a little bit dizzy."

At the jail, Murphy showed Travis's note to Christine and explained everything he knew and suspected. Finished, he unloaded the Smith by letting the bullets drop on top of the desk and sat down to clean the gun.

"What are you going to do?" Christine asked.

"First thing in the morning, I'm riding out to the Bar X."

"Alone?"

"That's what I figured."

"You can't go out there by yourself. Clyde and Sandy face the gallows for murder. They won't hesitate to kill you. Look what they've already done."

"I know, and I've given it a lot of thought. There's no way of knowing how many of Harrelson's hands will be at the ranch tomorrow or how loyal they are to him. Most of them are sure to know about the bootlegging and may be a part of it. If I go out there tomorrow with a posse and they fight us, I'll have a bloodbath on my hands. Several men on both sides will die, and I don't want that."

Murphy shoved a piece of oilcloth he'd taken out of a drawer through the bore of the revolver with a thin wooden dowel. "If I ride out there alone, Clyde and Sandy won't be alarmed by it. Once I get a gun on them, the hands will back off. If things work out right, I'll be back before dark with the both of them and no one gets hurt."

"And if *things* don't work out right?"

Murphy shrugged. "Part of the job, I guess." He smiled. "At least you'll get the dun back and the share you gave me in the store."

Christine raised her hand, and for a moment he was sure she was going to hit him. "If you're not back by dark, I'm sending Moses and every ranch hand I've got after you."

CHAPTER 19

CLYDE HARRELSON'S LARGE, two-story home stood like a giant sentinel over the miles of empty, grassy plains surrounding it. The flat-roofed adobe bunkhouse and barn a hundred yards or more to the side, by a cluster of corrals, seemed tiny in comparison, though they were bigger than most Murphy had seen.

Murphy held the dun in a slow walk as he passed through the gate. He purposely had taken his time getting to the ranch, not wanting to arrive too early and appear too eager. He guessed the time to be around ten.

A couple of shirtless men were by a large wood pile, splitting stumps. They stopped their work and watched him ride by. Another man in front of the barn was shoeing a horse and a few more were by the corrals, setting new cedar fence posts.

Murphy stopped in front of the house and dismounted. A brown-colored cur met him, yapping excitedly and snapping at his heels. Murphy kicked at him, barely missing.

A door slammed. "Shut it up, June."

The dog put her tail between her legs and headed for her master. Clyde Harrelson, dressed in a tan suit, no tie, and wearing a gun belt, walked down the wide veranda steps toward Murphy.

Murphy hadn't seen him since the night of the lynch party and he wondered about the reception he was about to get.

"Good mornin', Sheriff." Clyde stuck out his short, thick arm. "What brings you out this way?"

For a split second Murphy couldn't decide whether to draw and put the muzzle of the Smith in Clyde's belly or shake hands with him. He chose the latter. It seemed he had plenty of time to make the arrest and he needed to know where Sandy was. If he could get the two of them together, and get a gun on them, his job would be a lot easier.

"Rustling." Murphy wrapped the reins around the white hitching rail. "A couple of the ranches this side of Turrett have lost several head and I came out to see if you'd lost any, or had any ideas on it."

The tense lines in Clyde's face relaxed. "Haven't heard a thing about it. Haven't lost a cow as far as I know. I'm glad you came by though, I've been meaning to go to town and see you. I heard you got the Apaches that hit the Price place."

Clyde looked down. "I want to apologize for the other night at the jail. I was drinkin' too much and mad, too. I shouldn't have bucked you the way I did."

Murphy watched Clyde carefully, and if he hadn't already known better, he'd swear the man was sincere. Harrelson was no fool. He was smooth—very smooth.

"Don't worry about it. Whiskey's good at making men do things they shouldn't. I've had my share of regrets because of it." Murphy took out his sack of Durham. "Would Sandy be around?"

Clyde raised his head a little too fast, showing a touch of apprehension. "No, he's—he rode out early this mornin' to check on the boys at one of the line shacks. You know how they are. If you don't keep an eye on them, they won't work. What would you be needin' him for?"

"Nothing really." Murphy finished rolling his cigarette and licked the edge of the paper. "I just thought he might have heard something about the rustling he hadn't mentioned to you. Any piece I can get is more than I have. When do you think he'll get back?"

"May be a few days." Clyde looked up at the sky. "Looks like another grass burner and no rain. The country's goin' to get so dry it'll blow away." He gestured toward the house. "This heat makes me thirsty. Come on in and have a drink with me before you go."

"Sounds good." Murphy struck a match on the pipe rail and lit his cigarette, then followed Clyde inside. He wished Sandy were here and wasn't convinced that Clyde was telling the truth about him, yet there was nothing to be done about it. He had Harrelson, and if he could get him handcuffed out of sight of the ranch hands, so much the better.

They turned out of the entrance foyer into a large room filled with hunting trophies. Lion, bear, deer, elk, bobcat, and antelope hides covered the furniture, walls, and ceiling. Several heads were mounted. Clyde moved toward a short, cherrywood bar positioned in a corner. "Have a seat."

Murphy pulled the Smith and closed the door. Clyde turned at the sound, shocked to see the muzzle of the gun pointed at him. "What is this? What do you think you're doing?"

"Don't move, Clyde. Drop your gun belt."

"You're out of your mind. I—"

"Drop it! Do it now."

Clyde fumbled at the buckle a moment and let the gun belt fall to the floor. "You won't get away with this. Not here, not in my own house."

Murphy let the butt of his cigarette drop to the wood floor. He put his boot on it and twisted it out. "Yes, I will. I'm arresting you for the murder of Ben Simson, Travis Price, and his family." Murphy reached in his rear pocket for one of the two pairs of handcuffs he'd placed there before riding through the ranch gate.

"You really are insane. You know good and well that I shot Simson in self-defense. You talked to Sandy. He saw it."

"Clayton lied and so did you. Now turn around and put your hands behind your back. Go slow—real slow."

Clyde started around. "You're going to regret this. My men will kill you before you can get on your horse."

Murphy stepped toward him. "Maybe, but if you don't stop them, you'll die with me."

Keeping the Smith in his right hand, he used his left to clasp the handcuff around Clyde's wrist. He was about to handcuff the other hand when he heard the door open.

Murphy whirled to see smoke belch from Sandy Clayton's gun. As he pulled the trigger on the Smith, a slug hit him high in the chest next to his collarbone, knocking him down.

Sandy's gun boomed again, and Murphy felt a bullet hit his leg. He rolled to the side and another shot roared. He made it to his knees and swung the Smith in both hands to the doorway. Clayton was barely visible through the thick gun smoke. Three times Murphy pulled the trigger, shooting double-action. Clayton's gun went off, then dropped from his hand as he fell backward into the hall.

A shot exploded from the side and a bullet grazed the back of Murphy's head. He dropped to the floor and spun like a top on his belly, throwing a quick one-handed shot at Clyde, who stood a few feet from him. Clyde staggered, raised his revolver, and Murphy pulled the trigger on the Smith twice more. The second time the gun clicked empty.

Clyde fell face forward, hitting the floor with a loud thud. Quickly Murphy scrambled to his feet, reaching for the cartridges in his gun belt. His leg didn't bother him, didn't even feel like it had been hit, but the top, right quarter of his chest felt like it was gone, blown away.

He shoved one cartridge after another in the gun. Clyde groaned on the floor. His voice was weak and raspy. "I didn't kill them. Sanchez wasn't . . . wasn't suppose to hurt them. Only Travis. I never hurt no kid, never . . ."

Clyde lay quiet. Fast, heavy footsteps sounded on the

wooden steps outside. Murphy closed the loading hatch on the Smith, pulled the hammer back, and hurried into the foyer, stepping over Sandy Clayton's twisted, bloody body.

Through the glass panes in the front door he could see several of the ranch hands coming. One of them, a man with a stubble of a beard and thick, black sideburns, burst through the door, carrying a rifle.

Murphy fired the Smith, aiming high. "Stop! I don't want to kill you. Drop the gun."

The cowboy hesitated, noticed Clayton's body, then let the rifle slip from his hands. The men behind him on the veranda froze.

Murphy stepped toward him. "Turn around." He put the muzzle of the Smith against the back of the cowboy's head, suddenly feeling dizzy and weak. He shouted at the group through the open door.

"Listen to me. Harrelson murdered Ben Simson and he had the Price family killed. It was him or Clayton who finished off Travis in town.

"Now I don't want any trouble with any of you. I'm walking out. Don't do anything foolish or this man dies first."

Murphy pushed the cowboy out, keeping the Smith at his head. The ranch hands parted, making room for the two to walk. No one spoke. Murphy made it off the steps to the ground, half expecting at any moment to hear the report of a gun and feel the impact of a bullet in his back.

He reached the dun and lowered the Smith. "Untie him and put the reins over his neck, then face the house."

The man did as he was told. The other men, still on the porch, didn't move. Murphy wondered as he put his foot in the stirrup whether he had enough strength to mount the horse.

He grabbed the saddle horn with his left hand and in one mighty, painful motion swung into the saddle. The dun turned of his own accord and Murphy wildly kicked him. Faster and faster the horse ran, making it out the ranch gate in seconds with his rider barely hanging on.

CHAPTER 20

SKEET SET HIS coffee cup on the table. He and Moses had just finished eating lunch with Christine and Jenny at the store.

"Durn' fool stunt, him goin' off to the Bar X by hisself. I don't know why he's so blasted dumb. Don't he know he ain't the only one what's got a gun and knows how to use it?

"Why they prob'ly done filled him full of holes and dumped him in a gully somewhere to rot. Bet that'll teach him to use his head better the next time. He—"

"Skeet," Christine interrupted, "I told you. Al thought if he went alone it might avoid needless bloodshed."

"Hogwash. He just wanted to go off by hisself like he always does."

Moses wiped his mouth with a napkin, pushed his chair back, and stood. "I be goin' on out thataway. Shoulda done left. If Al gets them two men, I'll meet him on his way back. If he don't, he may be needin' help. No use in me waitin' around here."

Christine looked up at him, thinking he was right. Murphy should have arrived at the Bar X two or three hours ago. Whatever had happened there was probably over by now, and waiting until dark served no purpose.

It would take four hours to reach the Bar X. If Murphy had his prisoners, they would meet him along the way. If they didn't, he was likely in trouble.

"Saddle my mare too, Moses. We'll stop by the ranch and take any of the hands who are around with us."

Skeet shoved his chair back. "Now you're talkin'. 'Bout

time, too. I'll get my scattergun. Them boys at the Bar X better not mess around with me or I'll pepper the fool out of 'em."

"You can't go, Skeet. Your side—"

"Ah, ain't nothin' but a scratch. I can ride, I'm tellin' you. Why, I was ridin' 'fore you was born . . ."

Christine looked at Jenny, who sat quietly beside her. "Will you be all right? I want you to stay here, rest, and make yourself at home."

"I'll be fine. You've been so kind. I'm glad you're going. You've been worried sick all morning."

"It shows that bad, uh?"

Jenny rose, a knowing smile on her face. "I'll do these dishes."

Christine, Moses, Skeet, and six McCormick cowboys rode past the Price place on their way to the Bar X. An hour later and a little over halfway there, Moses pointed ahead to a small meadow between two short, timbered ridges. "It's Al's horse."

In moments the group reached the dun. Christine and Moses swung down. Dried blood covered the fork and seat of Murphy's saddle. Skeet, mounted on a mule, rode past them. He soon stopped. "Here he is."

Skeet dismounted and Christine ran toward him, followed by Moses and the other men. Murphy lay on his back, his eyes closed. Skeet raised up from the body.

"He's . . . he's dead."

Christine laid her head on Murphy's bloody chest and listened for a heartbeat.

Nothing.

She raised up. "Stop your horses! Be still. I can't hear."

Again she listened, hearing a faint, erratic heartbeat. "He's alive. Bring me my saddlebags and a canteen. Some of you stand around close to shade him. Hurry!"

His eyelids fluttered, as if he could hear what was going on.

She saturated a cloth bandage she'd packed, opened his lips with her fingers, and let it drip into his mouth, then softly wiped his face. Moses knelt beside him. "I don't know if you can hear me, but I be goin' to the Bar X. They gonna pay for this."

"I'm goin' too," Skeet said.

Murphy slowly shook his head. His whisper was barely audible. "Clyde . . . Sandy . . . they're dead."

Moses rose. "We better get him to the Doc's."

"We can't," Christine replied. "I'm afraid he'll die if we move him. He's too weak. Bring Doc Woods here."

She looked up at the men blocking the evening sun. "One of you build a fire and boil some water. Skeet, take a man with you to the ranch and load a packhorse with blankets, tarps, and food. Tell Sarah what's happened. She'll know what to send."

"Ain't gonna do it." Skeet spit a stream of tobacco juice to the side. "I'm bringin' the chuck wagon. I can get it here, you know. Nobody else could, but I can."

"Then quit talking and do it. Move!"

Christine stroked Murphy's forehead and cheeks with the wet bandage. She wasn't positive, but she thought she saw the start of a smile cross his lips.

CHAPTER 21

THREE MONTHS LATER, on Christmas day, Murphy, Christine, Skeet, Sarah, and Billy climbed in a wagon parked in front of the mercantile. Moses rode up on his huge buckskin. "It be kind of a cold day to go on a picnic."

"It'll be fun," Christine said. Her breath fogged. "We'll build a fire and make hot chocolate."

"Yeah, Moses," Billy said excitedly. "You're going to like it."

Skeet popped the reins and the two mules leaned into their harness. Murphy winced at the sudden jolt. Christine noticed it and placed her hand in his. "Are you going to be all right?"

Murphy smiled. "I'm fine. Just a little sore. I wouldn't miss this for anything."

It was noon when Skeet stopped the wagon beside a stream in a grassy sixty-acre flat below the Price homestead. Everyone in the wagon rose and faced Moses.

"Merry Christmas!"

"What? What you all be doin'?"

Billy jumped out. "It's yours, Moses." The boy spun around on his heels with his arms out. "All of it's yours."

Moses slowly dismounted and looked around him, obviously confused. Christine climbed out of the wagon and stepped beside him, her face beaming. "Each one of us chipped in to help Travis's sister, Jenny, go back east. She was heir to the Price ranch and she signed it over to us. We want you to have it."

Murphy moved to the end of the wagon bed and let his feet hang off. "I don't know much about farming, Moses, but the land looks good. The dirt's black, and if you could figure out how to spread the water, there's a lot of it. We thought maybe some of your relatives in Alabama might want to come up and give it a try."

Moses wiped his eyes with the back of his hand. He couldn't speak.

"Well," Skeet said, standing by the mules. "You all gonna just stand there and have me unhitch, build a fire, and do everythin'? That's the trouble with young folks. They ain't got no respect for their elders. They won't work, won't help, won't do nothin'. Just stand around.

"Why I remember . . ."

If you have enjoyed this book and would like to receive details about other Walker and Company Westerns, please write to:

Western Editor
Walker and Company
435 Hudson Street
New York, NY 10014